Stealing Magic

THE LEGACY OF ANDROVA

ALEX C. VICK

ISBN: 1539743462
ISBN-13: 9781539743460

Dedication

For Isabella, who read this first.

Contents

Prologue

This first bit might seem like it has nothing to do with you. It might seem unbelievable, or impossible. Trust me when I tell you that you need to know this. Even if you don't believe it at first.

A very long time ago, hundreds of years in our past, a treaty was signed between two worlds. The first, Androva, was the older of the two worlds, and its people were patient and changed little with the passing years. The second world, Terra, being younger, was more unsettled. Its people were still learning and always seeking out progress.

The treaty was agreed upon in order to defeat an evil that threatened the two worlds. One of the worlds was required to make a great sacrifice in order to defeat the evil. The other world, through the treaty, would honour that sacrifice and ensure the protection of both worlds forevermore.

This worked very well for a long time. Until a magic-taker by the name of Jax accidentally broke the treaty. Well, I say accidentally... it was pretty deliberate actually. And this is the story of how it all happened.

1 The Beginning

"She can't hear us," came the voice. "Look, she sleeps. And besides, I've never been caught before." It was a boy's voice, clear and confident in the quiet of the afternoon. "The portal will stay open for me, anyway. My spellstation is stronger than yours."

Shannon froze, her breath catching in her throat for the longest moment as she tried to keep utterly still. Portal? Spellstation? Lying under the chestnut tree at the edge of her garden, she had been somewhere between awake and asleep, trying to forget the weekend homework that was waiting for her inside the house. The warmth of the spring sunshine had settled on the afternoon like a blanket, with only the hum of a hard-working bumblebee to disturb her daydreaming.

Shannon was an intelligent girl, despite the occasional difficulties she experienced in applying herself to her homework. But she could only think of two possible ways to explain what she had just heard.

Either someone had gone to the trouble of silently breaking into her garden to play a kind of elaborate practical joke on her, or she was hearing the voice of an actual alien who had travelled here using a portal and a spellstation.

Both of those options seemed extremely unlikely. The first because she lived on an ordinary housing estate and could not imagine anyone she knew taking the trouble to act out such a far-fetched game. And the second because although she had read a lot of books in her thirteen years, and was particularly drawn to fantastical stories about other worlds, she was not crazy enough to believe that anything like that actually happened in real life.

"Jax, you can't," came a second voice. "We have to go back, you know the rules."

This boy's voice was higher and sharper, and not confident like the first voice. Shannon wondered if she were dreaming. That might be the most logical explanation. She carefully pressed her thumbnail hard into the tip of her forefinger in an attempt to find out. It hurt. So either her dream was extremely lifelike, or she really was awake.

"Rules were made to be challenged, Darius,"

came the first voice again. "These rules are hundreds of years old—has anyone ever tested them? As long as we are not actually seen, does it matter if one of the Terrans is physically present?"

"*What?*" gasped Darius. "You're crazy! She could open her eyes at any moment! If that happens it will be too late, and not even you will be able to stop the consequences. I should never have agreed to this."

Shannon could hardly believe her ears. The temptation to open her eyes was overwhelming. It was only lessened by the real panic she could hear in Darius's voice as he mentioned the mysterious "consequences" that would arise if she did so.

Either these boys were very good actors, or they really did believe they were from another world. And what was a "Terran"? Was that supposed to be *her?* There was a short silence. Shannon's heart was beating so fast, she was worried they would hear it over the sound of the tree's rustling leaves.

"I'll be quick," said Jax, in a much quieter, conciliatory voice this time. "Come on, Darius. If she didn't wake up while you were screaming at me like a girl just now, she's probably not going to wake up while we harvest the magic we need either."

"Alright." Darius sighed. "You've got five minutes, and then I insist we return."

"Longer than I need," replied Jax, some of the previous confidence creeping back into his voice.

Then all was quiet. Shannon strained to hear what was happening, while her mind struggled to make sense of their conversation..

Harvesting magic? There was no way to reasonably explain such a thing. Firstly, there was no such thing as magic. Yes, there were magic tricks that could be played, spectacles of illusion, but no actual real magic.

At the age of almost fourteen, Shannon no longer believed in the magical dreams of her childhood, like wizards and witches and fairy dust. If you pressed her, she would have to admit that she still looked for proof of magic, just every now and then, when she was feeling sentimental.

Of course, she had never found it. Yet here she was, listening to two boys who not only appeared to believe completely and matter-of-factly in magic, but intended to somehow harvest it from her garden.

Gradually she became aware of a change in the air around her. It stirred against her bare arms, almost making her shiver, and the temperature began to feel cooler, though the silence continued.

She felt some of the finer strands of her long

brown hair lifting up as though drawn by static electricity. Something was definitely happening. Her early disbelief gave way to nervousness. The silence was feeding her fear, and the skin on her face tingled as her panic grew.

But as the terror rose, she began to feel something else as well. The air was almost buzzing, and to her surprise, Shannon realised that it felt ever so slightly familiar. Like an echo of a memory. Her usually solemn brown eyes gleamed beneath their closed lids.

Meanwhile the internal debate continued to play out inside her mind. She actually wanted to open her eyes now.

But what if something terrible happened? Her family was inside the house, and though she didn't always see eye to eye with her parents and younger sister, she definitely did not want to bring "consequences" down on their heads.

Darius had made these consequences sound quite ominous. On the other hand, what if she missed her chance, and in five minutes Jax and Darius disappeared forever, never to return?

Shannon was mostly a well-behaved girl. There was a good chance that after considering her dilemma a little longer, she would keep her eyes shut and stay still. Eventually she could forget this strange interlude and convince herself that it really had all been a peculiar dream. However, on this occasion, that was not what happened.

Though she would not fully recognise it, or understand it, until a lot more time had passed, Shannon was no longer exactly the same person as she had been before the arrival of Jax and Darius.

There was a small spark deep inside her mind that had just been ignited. It is too soon in the story to explain exactly what the spark was, and more importantly why it was, but that spark tipped the balance in the argument Shannon was having with herself. She started to open her eyes.

At first she only opened them the tiniest amount, not knowing what to expect. Slowly she turned her head to the side where the voices had been coming from.

The first thing she noticed was the brightness. She could not open her eyelids any further until she became accustomed to the light. Everything was gleaming, as if lit from within. The sun in the sky paled into insignificance against the radiance of the energy coming from the grass, the trees, and the spring flowers. Every living part of the garden was glowing.

Cautiously Shannon sat up and extended a hand towards the trunk of the chestnut tree. As her fingers brushed against the light coming from the tree, it was like touching a magnetic field, and she could feel its power from the roots of her hair to the tips of her toes.

She took a slow breath to steady herself. Suddenly she remembered the two boys. She looked out into the garden again, and somehow she could open her eyes completely this time. It was as if while her hand rested in the light of the tree, she was part of it, and protected from the dazzling glare.

Strands of light were being drawn to the centre of the garden, where Shannon could make out two shadowy figures. They are boys after all! she thought, surprised. She was relieved that these aliens (for what else to call beings from another world?) were completely human-looking.

Though she was sensible enough to realise that outward appearances are no guarantee of character, it is of course easier to be brave when someone doesn't look like a monster.

While she watched, the figures became clearer as the strands of light gradually receded into a solid-looking silver ball held in the outstretched palm of the taller of the two. Shannon knew she only had a brief moment left before they saw her, so she tried to take in as many details as possible.

The boy holding the light had jet-black hair, long enough to brush his collar, and black clothes that looked incongruous in the heat of the afternoon. He had several freckles on his nose and a frown of intense concentration on his face, which shone pale in the glow of the light he was holding.

His shirt had a strange silver symbol on the top pocket. It was a seven-pointed star, with a spinning whirl in its centre that seemed to have no end or beginning. The closer she looked at it, the more it drew her in. As if it were trying to hypnotise her to fall into its spinning centre.

"Jax, we have to leave NOW!" gasped the other boy. Shannon glanced at him quickly. He was blond and dressed very similarly, but the symbol on his shirt was different, and definitely not spinning.

Jax looked up from the ball of light in his palm, and his green eyes met Shannon's. His mouth curved in a mischievous, but slightly mocking grin. "Thank you for the magic!" he said with a wink. Then he turned and both boys disappeared into thin air.

Immediately the light being generated by the garden vanished. It was so instantaneous that Shannon recoiled, sitting back on her heels as if she had been pushed. She looked all around her, but literally nothing remained to show that Jax and Darius had been there only a moment before. All the trees and plants looked as ordinary and familiar as ever.

Tentatively Shannon reached out to touch the trunk of the chestnut tree again. She felt the roughness of the bark under her fingers, but nothing else. She looked across at her house, and it also seemed entirely unchanged. So much for the famous "consequences," she thought.

She stood up on slightly wobbly legs and tried to concentrate. Was that ball of light somehow supposed to be made of magic? Shannon had never imagined that magic might be something that you could actually see or even hold. She half laughed to herself. I did see it, she thought. I even touched it! Her smile grew wider.

However, Darius had been right when he had spoken his warning. Shannon had seen him and Jax, and it *was* now too late.

2 Dangerous Thoughts

"What makes a good magician into a great magician?" asked the man.

"Discipline," replied Jax, mechanically.

"*Yes!*" said the man, raising his voice and slamming his fist onto the table. Jax looked up, only half interested, as he was very familiar with his father's opinions and the energy with which they were often expressed.

Revus was a strong man, tall and black-haired like his son, but with streaks of grey bisecting the black, a testament to his advancing years. Both their shirts displayed the same symbol, a seven-pointed star. Revus was a serving member on Androva's Council, and determined that his son should follow in his footsteps one day.

Father and son were in the dining chamber of Mabre House, the family's main residence. It was an imposing building, built out of grey rock, with black window frames and a very steep slate roof.

The forbidding theme continued inside, with little frivolity to be found in any of the furnishings. It suited Revus extremely well.

"Jax, are you paying attention?" Revus asked, even louder than before. "I do not remind you of this requirement because I enjoy repeating myself. Our society only survives because our magicians *follow the rules*. The danger that can and will arise from undisciplined magic is more serious than you can possibly comprehend."

The threat of these words, delivered as they were with absolute sincerity and conviction, should have given Jax pause for thought. However, he had heard them so many times throughout his life, over and over, that they had lost their ability to impress.

"Yes, Father," he said automatically.

"You could be a great magician," said Revus. "Maybe even greater than me." At this he allowed a small smile to lift the corners of his mouth.

He was not an unkind man, but since the death of his wife when Jax was only three years old, his naturally sombre bearing and strict disposition had been given free rein. Jax, having inherited a sense of mischief from his mother, found that he was increasingly tempted to resist the authority so sternly imposed on him by his father.

"Jax, if you make another trip to Terra during daylight hours, I will have no choice but to revoke your harvesting privileges. I cannot enforce the Code if my own son refuses to follow it. There is nothing more to be said on the matter."

He arose from his chair and looked down at his son, exasperated. He had spoken truthfully. Jax was the most promising magician in his class, as Revus had been before him. Not to mention that Jax was the best magic-taker in Androva's history. But he could not make allowances for this blatant disregard of the Code they all lived by. It was a miracle that there had been no consequences this time.

"Father?" asked Jax quietly as Revus turned to leave.

"Yes?" answered Revus impatiently.

"What happens if the rules are not followed? Everyone always speaks of the danger, but no one will tell me exactly what it is."

"You are too young." Revus sighed. "Not until the end of your eighteenth year can you be entrusted with the knowledge. You know this. Why do you continue to ask?"

Jax shrugged his shoulders. Revus shook his head and left without saying any more, as he had a Council meeting to attend that afternoon. It was an extra meeting that had been called to discuss the authorisation of some additional harvesting trips.

Jax, alone in the room, felt his spirits lift with the departure of his father. He had not really expected Revus to answer his question. He knew from snippets of information that he and his best friend, Darius, had overheard while growing up that the Code was something to do with a treaty of utmost importance and secrecy going back hundreds of years.

Magicians who were of age spoke about it only in hushed tones and behind closed doors. Jax had harboured a small hope that his recent daylight trip to Terra might force his father to reveal why the rules of the Code were so important.

Part of him did believe, as he had told Darius, that he was right to challenge rules that had remained the same for hundreds of years. But another part of him was simply fed up with not knowing.

He amused himself by creating a small spell to clear the table, lining up the dishes and cutlery and making them march up and down until they crashed off the edge onto the stone floor. Suddenly bored with the game, he repaired the dishes and returned to his chair to think.

Despite his outward air of teenage indifference, he had in fact been feeling something when Revus had lectured him yet again on following the rules. It was not guilt, or fear, or even nervousness (all reasonable feelings given the warning in his father's words). It was instead burning curiosity.

His thoughts had returned constantly in the past few days to the Terran he had encountered with Darius on their most recent harvest. He had not told Darius, but he had seen her before. That particular garden yielded a very impressive amount of magic.

Ever since Jax had first discovered it, one night nearly a year ago, he had made return trips. Magic-takers did not revisit the same place too often, in order to give the Terran magic a chance to replenish itself, but Jax had visited four times now.

It was during the visit before this most recent one with Darius that he had seen the Terran girl. It had been the dead of night, as usual, and his portal companion had taken suddenly ill.

Underage magicians were prohibited from travelling to Terra alone—the portals would not allow it, no matter how superior the magician and his or her spellstation. But when his companion on that trip, a magician called Bellis, had been forced to return early, Jax was left by himself to complete the harvest and travel back with the magic.

He could not understand afterwards what

made him do it. Even for a naturally curious magician with a healthy disrespect for authority, seeking out a Terran was a very big deal. After all, testing the rules was one thing, but deliberately smashing them to pieces was something else altogether.

He had been shocked to notice a faint light emanating from one of the windows of the house, and he knew he could not continue with collecting the magic if there was any risk of being observed. He could not believe that he and Bellis had not noticed the light when they arrived.

The correct thing would have been to return to Androva immediately, of course. But Jax did not do that. It crossed his mind, for the very briefest of instants, but was never seriously considered as a course of action.

He was confident in his ability to manage the situation, and he did not wish to return to Androva without his harvest of magic. It was not just a matter of pride. There was a quota that Androva had to meet regarding the quantity of magic harvested each month. Jax rose to the window and cautiously peered above the sill.

There is so much unused magic on Terra that it is possible for a magician with even the most basic of training to pretty much do whatever he or she wishes. That is why the trips to Terra by underage magicians are so carefully controlled—

just imagine the possibilities otherwise.

Unfortunately for Council members like Revus, a magician's ability to harvest magic is strongest *before* he or she comes of age. So Revus had no choice but to allow teenagers like his son to travel to Terra as magic-takers. All the Council could do was reduce the risk by ensuring that solo travel was not permitted.

Therefore when Jax decided to rise up into the air, he did just that. Androvan magicians have no use for wands, hats, cloaks, magic words, or other such accessories. Their magical force field is a part of themselves and any green living thing around them, and requires only training to strengthen it and to learn how to apply it.

At first Jax could see nothing because there was a curtain across the inside of the window. He slowly moved his forefinger across the glass, and obligingly the curtain inside lifted slightly.

There was a girl lying on the bed inside the room, wearing purple pyjamas. She was resting on her elbows, reading a book. Her hair was brown and fell loose over her shoulders, and her profile showed that her eyebrows were raised in wonder at what she was reading. She was so focused on the book, there seemed no chance that she would look up and notice Jax.

He wondered at the attention she bestowed upon this book. She appeared to find it so fascinating that there was nothing else in the room that existed for her. He had never been so transfixed by a book himself, for on Androva, books exist only to relate history, the rules of the Code, and how to use magic.

Jax had never encountered the kind of book Shannon was reading—a modern fairy tale, with swooping highs and lows, and adventure, and no boundaries except the limits of the author's imagination. He stared at the girl, wishing with all his heart that he could see what was written on those pages that mesmerised her so completely.

Eventually, after a long moment had passed, he let the curtain fall back, returned to the garden, and collected the magic as planned. But what he had seen stayed in his mind, even after returning to Androva.

Jax had always felt superior to the Terrans. After all, they were not magicians, and apparently never would be, something which had always made him pity them. But being ignored by this girl in favour of a book, of all things, annoyed and intrigued Jax in equal measure. He could hardly wait until enough time had passed for the magic to replenish itself so that he could go back.

He managed to convince Darius to make a daylight trip, knowing the risk he was taking, but unable to resist finding out more about this Terran girl.

Darius and Jax had been friends nearly all their lives. Their fathers both worked for the Androvan government, Revus on the Council and Marek, Darius's father, in the Repository of Magic. Marek was one of the magicians tasked with protecting the stores of magic harvested from Terra. His wife, Iona, was a teaching magician who had a particular talent for prophecy.

Jax had always been the leader in his friendship with Darius, and both boys were content with this state of affairs. With Darius's tendency to moderation and Jax's tendency to take risks, they were usually able to strike a balance in the middle that benefited both of them.

Alone in the dining chamber, Jax reflected on what had happened when he and Darius had made that most recent trip to Terra. At first his feelings had been conflicted. There was disappointment that the girl had been seemingly oblivious to his presence once again, but also relief that, after all, he had not broken the first rule of the Code.

After agreeing on a five-minute time limit with Darius, he had then concentrated on harvesting as much magic as possible. The density of the ball of light as it formed in his palm had been remarkable—it was more magic than he had ever collected before. Then Darius had gasped his warning. Jax had looked up, and as he met the girl's brown eyes, he had realised two things.

Firstly, he realised that he could feel the symbol on his shirt spinning, something that should not happen, and in fact, could not happen until he was of age and had completed his training.

Secondly, he realised the girl was touching the tree, and some of the magic he was collecting was definitely coming from *her*.

3 Return To Terra

"Hey, Shannon, where did you get to this morning?" asked Penny irritably.

Shannon glanced up at the sound of Penny's voice. Penny was her best friend, and usually they walked to school together every morning. Shannon was in the school library, looking in the biggest, fattest dictionary she had been able to find on the shelves.

She'd hoped that it might tell her something better than what she had already found online. Staring down one last time to commit the information to memory, she turned to Penny, still half distracted.

"Sorry, I had to come to the library early to finish my homework," she explained.

"So why didn't you text me?" asked Penny.

"Sorry," said Shannon again. She could understand Penny's frustration. If their positions had been reversed, she would have been upset

with Penny.

But ever since the amazing events of the previous afternoon, she had been walking around in a kind of daze, not entirely sure how to go about her normal life after experiencing something so astonishing. Her mind returned again to the entry in the dictionary that she had just closed.

Consequence: a) Something that logically or naturally follows from an action or situation
b) A punishment or negative after-effect

She had been determined to double-check her understanding of what *consequences* actually meant, so she had come in early to the school library that morning. Darius had said it would be "too late" if she opened her eyes, and that consequences would follow.

Well, she had definitely opened her eyes. What she couldn't figure out was whether these consequences would be bad or good. The dictionary had not really helped because the definition seemed to suggest that a bad result was possible, but not necessarily certain.

Shannon had spent the rest of the day before in the garden, closely examining every tree and flower for signs of the magic light she had seen earlier (much to the delight of her father, who had never known her to take such an interest in his garden before). After it started to get dark, she had to admit defeat. She was starting to feel a bit silly anyway.

Later, when the house was finally silent for the night, she found it very difficult to get to sleep. She felt different, but she couldn't pinpoint exactly what it was. The spark that had ignited in her mind earlier was getting bigger, though Shannon didn't know this yet.

"Hello?" called Penny, waving her hand in front of Shannon's face. "Anyone home?"

"Sorry…" began Shannon, but Penny interrupted her.

"Oh, stop saying sorry. Let's go to registration. We might as well see what delights are waiting for us in double Maths."

Linking her arm with Shannon's, she pulled her in the direction of their classroom. Following Penny, Shannon decided to try to put Jax and Darius out of her mind for the rest of the school day. She would allow herself some time to think about them when she got home.

Penny looked at Shannon quizzically a couple of times, as if she knew something was different. Much like Jax and Darius, they had been friends for years, ever since both had started primary school together. This was their third year in secondary school, and they had settled in very well.

Penny was a similar height to Shannon, and also had long brown hair. However, Penny's blue eyes, wild curls, and her tendency to experiment with a different look nearly every day, meant that the two girls did not really look very much alike.

In personality, they were also very different. While Penny was a very practical person more interested in doing than thinking, Shannon was more of a dreamer. This might have caused arguments, but in fact the girls' friendship was very harmonious.

The next few days passed in a similar way, with Shannon trying to live her normal life as much as possible, while continuing to examine her memory of that Sunday afternoon whenever she had a spare moment.

She was finding the whole thing very frustrating because no matter how many times she went over it, there was no way to find the answers to any of her questions. She usually came up with more questions each time, which made her feel as if she were getting further and further away from any conclusion.

Where did the boys come from?

Why were they stealing magic, and why from her garden?

Would they ever come back?

What should she do if they did?

And how could she stand it if they *didn't?*

Each day passed more slowly than the previous one and sleeping continued to be difficult.

Quite apart from the endless questions, it was almost as if Shannon could feel a faint buzzing deep inside her head. If she concentrated very hard, as the week went by, she could make the buzzing travel down her arms, and by Thursday she had made it reach all the way to her fingertips.

Lifting her hands in front of her face, she wondered if it was her imagination or if they really were giving off a weak glow. The longer she stared at them, the less convinced she was.

"Oh, this is ridiculous," she said to herself crossly. "How much time have I wasted on this? And I'm getting nowhere!"

She had talked to no one about her meeting with Jax and Darius, or the whole magic light experience. Several times she was tempted to mention it to Penny, but she never did.

Knowing Penny so well, she could easily predict that Penny would think Shannon was making up the whole thing for a laugh. There were times when Shannon considered that she might have gone mad without knowing it. How would she know?

Deciding that the glow was in her imagination

after all, Shannon determined that she was going to get a good night's sleep for once, and she put all thoughts of portals, spellstations, and unsettling green-eyed stares from her mind.

It worked, and she awoke the next morning feeling better than she had all week. She kept her mind focused on school and normality all of Friday, and attacked her weekend homework that evening with a determination that surprised both her parents.

Of course, there was a reason why she was doing all of this. She secretly hoped that the weekend would bring a return of the two boys, and she wanted to have no distractions if it did.

Saturday dawned overcast and miserable. It was one of those chilly spring days that make everyone think summer is a long way off after all. Shannon's parents decided to take their daughters into the nearby town to buy new school shoes.

As she trailed after Tammy, her younger sister, and waited in the endless queue to have her seven–year-old sister's feet measured, Shannon felt like screaming with frustration. She took a photo of the shoe shop to send to Penny, typing **"Death by queueing :("**

Penny replied with **"Swap you, I have to do the DUSTING today. Death by housework."**

Shannon grinned and felt a bit better.

The next morning, it was still cloudy, and

Shannon spent some time finishing her homework before settling down with a new book. Gradually the skies cleared, and by lunchtime the sun was shining. Her parents chose to eat lunch outside, and Shannon started to feel nervous that the entire afternoon would pass without her having the chance to be in the garden on her own.

Eventually her father went back into the house to watch a football match and her mother took Tammy out for a ride on her new bike. They tried to persuade Shannon to come with them, but she refused, pretending that she had a bit more homework left to finish.

Finally, she was alone. Peace and quiet descended as the voices of her mother and sister travelled further away from the house. Shannon got up and walked to her favourite chestnut tree, then sat down with her back against its solid base.

The ground was a little damp from the rain the day before, but Shannon didn't mind. Tilting her head back, she closed her eyes and focused on the buzzing in her head.

Ever since her decision on Thursday evening to get a good night's sleep, she had discovered that she could switch off the buzzing, or concentrate on it, and magnify it as she chose. Here in the garden, surrounded by the trees and plants, and with nothing to disturb her concentration, it seemed to be stronger than ever.

Now it wasn't so much a buzzing—it felt more like a force field. In fact, it felt sort of similar to when she had touched the magic light radiating from the tree one week ago.

Shannon imagined the force field travelling down her arms to her fingertips again. She kept her eyes closed for the longest time, scared to open them in case she was dreaming the whole thing. Eventually she took a deep breath and opened her eyes.

"Wow!" she gasped. This time there was no mistaking it. Her hands were glowing. Just as before, it was not the same as the bright yellow light of the sun in the sky. It was a pure, clean silver colour, and Shannon was transfixed.

She moved her hands slowly back and forth in front of her, and they left a silver trail behind them. She experimented by drawing shapes, and these held their form for several seconds before dispersing. Gradually she became aware that the tree behind her was also buzzing with the same energy. Turning slightly, she reached out to touch the tree, and her hand tingled where it brushed against the dimly glowing bark.

"I *knew* it!" shouted the voice triumphantly.

Shannon nearly jumped out of her skin at the unexpected words. Abruptly the force field seemed to snap back inside her head, leaving her hands and the surface of the tree completely back to normal.

She scrambled to her feet to confront the owner of the voice, knowing already who it was.

"Jax, I presume?" she said as calmly as she could manage, though her heart was still jumping from the shock, and she was already half smiling in amazement at what was happening.

Jax, standing with his hands in his pockets, and smiling the same mischievous, slightly mocking grin that she remembered from last time, raised his eyebrows. "You have the advantage over me, Terran," he said. "I don't know your name."

"Shannon," she answered. "And you *knew* what, exactly?"

Jax gave a half-bow. "Pleased to meet you, Shannon. And I knew you were a magician."

Shannon's mouth fell open. Before she could reply, he continued.

"I shouldn't even be able to travel here on my own. You see this symbol on my shirt?"

He pointed to the star, the centre of which was spinning again just as it had the week before. "It wasn't until I met you that it started to spin. It's not supposed to be able to do that until I come of age. In *four years' time.*" He paused to make sure she understood the significance of this fact. "Who are you? Why is this happening?"

Shannon laughed. To think that Jax was the

one asking questions of her!

"I have a question for you," she responded. "It's about something I heard your friend Darius say. What will the consequences be, and should we be worried about them?"

They stared at each other, both realising that something important could be happening. "We won't find the answers on Terra," Jax declared. "You'll have to come back with me." He held out his hand.

Shannon paused for the longest moment. Then she made up her mind and took hold of his hand.

4 More Questions Than Answers

Shannon blinked. She had grabbed Jax's hand a split second before, taken three steps forward, and the world had changed. Quite literally, as it would turn out. They were in a small dark room with lots of symbols painted in various colours on the walls, floor, and ceiling.

She looked down and realised she was standing on a green circular mat that glittered and felt slightly rough under her feet. The air around them was shimmering gently, and as she watched, the shimmer retreated downwards, leaving the air clear. The mat no longer glittered, and was now a plain dark green colour.

"This," said Jax, gesturing downwards, "is my spellstation." He sounded very proud of something that, to Shannon, seemed rather ordinary. "Green is the most powerful colour," Jax continued. "And it's big enough to transport two magicians who are of age. No other magician as young as me has managed such a feat before."

Shannon tried to look impressed. Jax sighed. "I suppose you don't know anything about it," he said disappointedly. "You'll have to take my word for it then," he concluded with a hint of his former smile. "You will have to trust me on matters Androvan, and I will have to trust you on matters Terran."

"Androvan?" asked Shannon. "Androva? Is that where we are?"

"Yes," replied Jax. "At least, we are in one of the portal rooms in Mabre House, where I live, which is in our capital, Landor."

Shannon looked at Jax, surprised that she didn't feel more scared. She was nervous of course, but she was also proud of herself for keeping control and not letting her fear get the better of her. Where should she start? Which question to ask first? Before she could begin, Jax gestured to the door.

"We have to go somewhere else," he said. "There is nowhere to hide in here, and I have to make sure that you remain undiscovered while we figure this out."

Obediently, Shannon followed him through the door. They entered a corridor, also quite dark, and followed it to another door at the end. Through this door was a long flight of stairs, twisting round and round in a circle, upwards and upwards. Shannon felt like she had gone back in time to a medieval castle.

Eventually they reached the top, where it was much lighter. "The portal rooms have to be underground," whispered Jax. "It's not considered safe to travel from the surface." Shannon hurried after him, taking in as much of her surroundings as she was able to, and not thinking much of the owner's taste in pictures and furniture.

Eventually Jax stopped and opened a large wooden door. She followed him into the generously sized room, and her eyes widened. It looked like the room of a prince! The furniture was ornately carved, and the furnishings were, even to Shannon's uneducated eye, extremely luxurious.

The floor glinted with patterns that shifted under her feet, and the ceiling was covered with different-coloured clouds that moved to and fro, in a kaleidoscopic rainbow.

She turned her astonished face to Jax, and he shrugged. "I experiment a lot. I don't even know myself what some of these spells will eventually become."

Shannon walked to the large curved window and sat down on the ledge. For a moment, she looked out at the beautiful countryside, as picturesque as anywhere on her own world. Far in the distance, there was an imposing mountain that cast a shadow over its surroundings, but Shannon did not look at it too closely.

"The capital is in the other direction," offered Jax. "You can't see it from this side of the house." Shannon turned back to him and sighed. She felt very tired all of a sudden.

"Of course!" Jax exclaimed. "You need a Portal Remedy. Travel through the portal is exhausting the first few times you do it. I should have thought of that. I'm sorry."

He walked across to a table on the other side of the room and returned with a very small blue-coloured glass, which was full to the brim with liquid.

"Drink it," he urged, and Shannon took the glass suspiciously. She sniffed it, but it did not smell of anything. Her arms and legs were starting to feel as if they were weighed down with lead, so she decided she might as well risk it.

She closed her eyes, held her breath, and tipped the liquid down her throat. Despite her fears, it slid down like honey and was remarkably pleasant. Almost immediately, she felt her strength returning.

"Better?" asked Jax, and she nodded. He took the glass and sat down on the other side of the window ledge. They looked at each other. "Why do you—?" started Shannon, at the same time that Jax said. "How did you—?"

They both laughed nervously. "You go first," said Jax. "I've got a feeling I need to answer a few of your questions first before you can be any help answering mine."

"OK," replied Shannon. "Why do you travel to my world and steal its magic?" she began.

"Steal?" replied Jax, shocked. "Stealing magic is not what we do. We harvest it."

"You steal it," retorted Shannon. "If it's not stealing, why do you only do it in secret? And why does no one on my world seem to know that it's happening?"

"Exactly!" said Jax. "If you don't know it's happening, and you don't even know the magic is there in the first place, and you don't miss it when it's gone, how can it be stealing? Besides, it has always been this way. For hundreds of years magic-takers have travelled from Androva to Terra to harvest its magic."

"You still haven't answered my question," said Shannon, crossing her arms. "Why do you do it?"

Jax shifted in his seat and looked out of the window. "I don't exactly know why," he mumbled.

"What?" said Shannon.

"I don't know why!" repeated Jax, more loudly. His cheeks went a little red, and he scuffed his boot along the floor. "I am not permitted to know until I am of age. I only know that it has something to do with a very old treaty, and it's a really bad thing if Androva doesn't harvest its full magic quota each month.

"We have a Code of rules that has to be followed by everyone on Androva, and the first three rules, the most important three, relate to magic-taking."

Shannon frowned as she considered what Jax had said. "So there is at least some kind of reason behind why you do it. You're not just stealing and using the magic for entertainment."

"Harvesting," corrected Jax. Though he could sort of see Shannon's point of view about the whole stealing thing, he was determined that she should not think of him as a thief.

"Whatever," replied Shannon with a small smile. She uncrossed her arms and looked down at her hands.

"Let's try looking at this from a different angle," she said. "Why were my hands glowing?"

Jax smiled back. This question he could answer. "It's the magic force field that makes them glow," he began. "All magicians have a spark of magic inside them that ignites during their thirteenth year. It starts out small, but gradually the power increases until the magician can feel it. It begins like a kind of humming as the energy builds up. You feel it inside your head first, and then you can begin to direct it outwards."

"Yes!" interrupted Shannon, her face shining. "That's exactly what it felt like!"

Jax smiled more widely. He too remembered the amazement of discovery that Shannon was feeling. And he had known what to expect, he had been waiting for it. How much more extraordinary would it be if you were completely unprepared?

"Eventually it becomes strong enough to project spells with," he continued. "There are lots of different ability levels. You don't know for sure how powerful you'll be until you come of age.

"The training can help you to develop certain skills, but the basic magic ability that every magician has is not determined by his or her skill in the classroom. It is something you are born with," he declared.

"And the tree? And the rest of the garden?" questioned Shannon. "The tree was glowing too."

"All green living things produce some amount of magic," answered Jax. "Trees produce the most by far. The taller the better. But we don't have very many tall trees on Androva." Shannon looked out of the window again. She saw that Jax was right. There were no tall trees in the landscape at all.

"On Androva, the living magic is always used up because magic-making is a part of our lives every day. There are a lot of magicians on Androva and not enough magic to go around most of the time."

"So maybe that's why you take it from us?" responded Shannon, raising her eyebrows.

"No, the answer is not that simple," replied Jax. "All the magic we harvest from Terra is returned to the Repository of Magic. No withdrawals are permitted. I already told you, I don't know what it's used for." His voice was a bit annoyed as he continued. "We don't waste it. Didn't you believe me before?"

"I'm sorry," said Shannon. "I do believe you. I'm just trying to make sense of all of this." She looked down at her trainers, noticing that one of the laces was starting to come loose, and she bent down to retie it.

"Why did this happen to me? That whole thing you described about the magic spark… firstly, I already had my thirteenth birthday, so this is my fourteenth year, and secondly, this just doesn't happen on my world. Unless there's an entire conspiracy going on that I don't know about."

"There is no conspiracy," responded Jax. "Trust me, there are no magicians on Terra. There is a lot of living magic, but it's never used by anyone."

"OK then, why me?" repeated Shannon.

"I can't explain it," said Jax quietly. "But I can tell you that if you progressed in one week from your initial spark to being able to direct your magic outwards like that, then you are very powerful. It can take months to get that far."

"Really?" asked Shannon, feeling excited. She gave Jax a small mischievous smile. "More powerful than you?"

"No!" he replied instantly. Then he laughed. "It would be close though," he admitted. "We would have to put it to the test to know the answer."

"OK then," she said, standing up.

Jax looked at her, shocked.

"I'm kidding!" She smiled, sitting down again. "I might have totally lost my mind, because right now I do actually believe I'm on another world that happens to be full of magicians.

"But I'm not quite crazy enough to fight one of them."

"You're funny," he said. "Maybe we're both a bit crazy. This is not exactly a normal Sunday afternoon for me either." Then he frowned. "But we could do an experiment. We might as well find out for sure."

"Find out what?" asked Shannon.

"Find out how powerful you are," he answered.

Shannon stood up again and backed away from him, holding her hands up to ward him off. "Hey, I was joking before. I don't want to get into any kind of contest."

Jax pointed to her hands, which were giving off a silver glow. "I think your magic might disagree with you." He smiled. "Your natural defences are already kicking in. But I'm not going to fight you. I just want to find out if you can use it."

He walked towards the middle of the room, beckoning Shannon to follow him. When they were standing in the centre, where the ceiling was at its highest point, he said, "I want you to try to touch the ceiling. Don't worry about the clouds, those spells are not complete, so they can't hurt you."

Shannon stared at him. "What?" she exclaimed. "Are you mad? How could I possibly do that? I'm not tall enough to touch the ceiling!"

"I know that," responded Jax patiently. "I want you to lift yourself up to the ceiling using magic.

"Solo Transference is one of the most challenging spells that a new magician can perform. Most cannot do it without help. On Terra it's easy because there is so much unused living magic available. But here on Androva, it is very difficult."

His green eyes were solemn for once as they looked into hers. "Just try it," he urged.

5 The Code

Shannon closed her eyes. Suddenly she didn't need to ask Jax any more questions. It was as if the magic inside her knew what to do. Arms by her sides, she held out her palms flat towards the floor, keeping her fingers closed. "Up," she whispered, quietly but very firmly, keeping her eyes tightly shut. A few seconds passed, then she felt a hand on her arm.

"Open your eyes," said Jax. Shannon lifted both eyelids together, just a tiny amount. The first thing she saw was Jax's steady green-eyed gaze. She lifted her eyelids further, until her eyes were fully open. "Keep looking at me," encouraged Jax, "and keep concentrating," he continued.

Shannon's breathing was very fast, and her heart was beating even faster. Deliberately, she took a longer, slower breath in and relaxed her shoulders. Her mind was still repeating "Up, up, up."

"OK," said Jax, "why don't you try touching the ceiling now?"

Shannon's eyes widened. She looked above her head, and the clouds were right there! She gasped and immediately looked down, shocked at how far away from the floor she was. She moved her feet back and forth a few times, fascinated to see them travelling through thin air.

"Are you alright?" asked Jax. "Looking down at this point is not usually a good idea." He laughed.

"I'm OK," said Shannon slowly, a look of wonder on her face. It was quite terrifying, but also kind of exhilarating.

She looked back up at the clouds and tentatively lifted one of her hands from its downwards-facing position, half afraid that she might fall. But nothing happened. She reached up to the colourful clouds, swirling her fingers from left to right, feeling them tingle.

"Wow," she said finally. "Wow!"

"I'm impressed," said Jax. "Most magicians fall the first time."

She looked across at him, still almost unable to believe they were having a conversation while floating high up by the ceiling. "Did you fall?" she asked curiously. There was a pause.

"Yes," he answered reluctantly. Then he

smiled. "But I only fell for a second, so it doesn't really count."

Shannon smiled back. At this moment she was so amazed and happy, she didn't really care if Jax had fallen or not, and she certainly wasn't going to argue about it.

Turning back to the ceiling, she discovered that if she paid close attention, she could almost hear the clouds talking to her, whispering their spells along a current of energy that travelled up from her fingertips. It was all completely mind-blowing.

She faced Jax again, suddenly remembering the silver symbol on his shirt. The centre of the star was not moving. She stared at it, then reached out with her hand as if to touch it. It began to spin, slowly at first and then faster and faster the closer she got. She moved her hand back, and the spinning slowed down again. "Tell me what that means," she demanded. "What is it for, and why does it spin like that?"

Jax reached out and rested his hands on Shannon's shoulders, and gradually, they descended to the ground. He looked at her seriously. "I will tell you as much as I know," he sighed. "Let's sit down again." They walked back to the windowsill and returned to their former positions. Shannon looked back up at the ceiling, still absorbing what had just happened. This was turning into the most unbelievable day of her life. She turned back to Jax expectantly, and he started to talk.

"This symbol is my family Sygnus," he began. "Each bloodline of magicians on Androva has their own Sygnus, and they have existed for hundreds of years. There are fifty in total, and each one is quite different. When two bloodlines join together in marriage, one must adopt the Sygnus of the other. The chosen Sygnus is decided by the Council."

"The Council?" asked Shannon. "What's that?"

Jax looked at her, realising again how little she knew about his world. On Androva, the Council was everything. Nothing happened without the Council knowing about it. Nothing was permitted without the Council's agreement.

"The Council are in charge of everything," he tried to explain. "They have absolute power over every magician on Androva. The Council enforce the Code."

Shannon swallowed. Suddenly her mouth was very dry. "I somehow don't think they'd be very happy about me," she managed.

Jax thought for a moment. "My father is a senior Council member," he admitted. Shannon made a shocked sound and started to speak, but Jax interrupted her.

"I think we are safe for now. He never comes to my rooms, and a just a week ago he reprimanded me for my daylight trip to Terra. He would not imagine that I would be testing the rules again so soon," he finished with a wry smile.

"I have no choice but to trust you," said Shannon. "But I still don't like the sound of the Council."

"I'm not their biggest fan either," responded Jax. "But remember, we do not mean Androva any harm, we are only trying to understand what is happening."

"That's true," said Shannon, nodding. "You'd better carry on then."

Jax continued. "Each magician adopts the Sygnus of his or her family when training begins. It is traditionally the first spell you project, the spell which engraves your family Sygnus onto the shoulder of every shirt or jacket you ever wear. It is part of your identity."

"What about the spinning then?" said Shannon, leaning forward. "You said that only happens when you grow up?"

"Yes," agreed Jax. "The Sygnus is also a key. When you come of age, you are able to activate the key and unlock certain spells that are off limits to underage magicians. Spells like travelling alone through the portal. When the key is activated, the centre of your Sygnus starts to spin."

Shannon was quiet for a moment as she absorbed this information, twirling a strand of hair around her fingers, something she often did to help her think.

"Yours doesn't spin all the time though?" she checked.

"No," responded Jax. "I had great difficulty in getting it to spin again for my trip to Terra earlier today. It took a lot of magic. It is actually fortunate that it does not spin so easily: otherwise, my father would certainly have noticed."

"What about this Code?" Shannon asked finally. "I wanted to know about the 'consequences' Darius mentioned. Something tells me that they could be really important."

"I am not of age, remember," said Jax, shaking his head in frustration. "I have no information for you about the exact nature of these consequences."

"But do you know if they are bad?" continued Shannon.

Jax paused as he considered whether he should answer her question honestly. Eventually, he sighed, realising that there was not much point continuing if they were not going to be truthful with each other. "Yes," he replied.

"Yes, you know, or yes, they are bad?"

Shannon pressed him.

"They are bad," he confirmed.

Shannon looked down at her knees. Part of her had already known what he would say. "I think I knew that," she said quietly.

Jax got up and walked across to a large bookcase. He took down a slim volume that was dark green in colour and embossed with elaborate gold letters. He turned the book so Shannon could see what was written on the front of it:

The Code

He held the book out to Shannon, and she took hold of it extremely carefully. "It's alright," said Jax, smiling. "It won't break. Books on Androva are self-repairing, look." He lifted it out of her hands, deliberately tore several pages out of the middle, and dropped them on the floor.

As Shannon watched, the pages flew back up again and inserted themselves back into the book, which then shut itself rather abruptly.

"I don't think it liked that," said Shannon, quite shocked, but half laughing as well. She reached out and took the book back, running her fingers over the gold letters. Then she opened the cover and started to read.

1. *When travelling to Terra, each Androvan magician shall take all precautions necessary*

to ensure that his or her presence is unknown,
unsuspected, and undetected by any Terran

2. No underage magician is permitted to travel to
Terra unaccompanied

3. The Council shall enforce all necessary
measures to collect the harvest quota in full,
each month **without fail**

4. There will be fifty permitted Sygnus images
according to the ancient bloodlines, and when
two families join in marriage the Council
shall determine which Sygnus prevails

5. Each magician shall attend five full years of
training before coming of age

6. No underage Sygnus activation is permitted,
and accordingly the Council will project
universally preventive spells

7. Each magician at the end of his or her
eighteenth year, will attend the coming of age
ceremony and graduate to a lifetime
profession selected by the Council

8. The Council will maintain the Register of

Unauthorised Spells and will also determine the appropriate punishment for any transgression

9. Repeated breaches of the Code will not be tolerated, and the Council may apply the Spell of Removal in extreme cases

10. The Council shall consist of twenty elected members, each with equal authority, and each serving for a maximum of ten years before re-election

By the time she reached the end of the list, Shannon's face had turned quite white. "You weren't joking about the influence of the Council, were you?" she said weakly. "Exactly how many rules have we broken?"

"Oh, only about three or four, no big deal," said Jax, trying to look like he didn't care.

"What is the Spell of Removal?" asked Shannon. Jax immediately stopped smiling. "It removes your spark," he answered in a low voice. "And it is permanent. No more magic. Ever."

Shannon closed the book, unwilling to read any more. She was starting to feel very tired again, overwhelmed with the excitement and anxiety of the past few hours. Suddenly she got to her feet.

"What time is it?" she asked urgently.

"I don't know," replied Jax. "Near to sundown I would imagine." Shannon recoiled. "I have to get back!" she said. "My parents will be going crazy!"

"OK, calm down," said Jax. "Let me think for a moment. There might be a way…"

"What?" said Shannon impatiently.

"I've never tried it, but since this is a day for first times, we might as well see if it works."

"*What?*" repeated Shannon.

"The portal is supposed to have a memory," explained Jax. "It means that we could theoretically make the same trip that I made earlier today, arriving on Terra in the same location at the exact same time.

"I've never done it, because it's advanced magic. But it might work now that my Sygnus is activated. It's risky though."

Shannon narrowed her eyes, trying to think what to do for the best. Then she decided that she had nothing to lose, so she nodded. "OK, let's try it," she said.

Jax quickly checked that all was still quiet in the corridor outside his room, and then he and Shannon ran back the way they had come. They didn't stop until they were outside the door to the portal room again, both a bit out of breath.

"OK," he said, "here we are." They re-entered the room, and Jax pulled Shannon forwards until both were standing on the spellstation. Shannon watched as Jax raised the palm of his right hand to several of the symbols on the walls around them in sequence, one after another, noticing how they each lit up in turn. Finally he lifted his hand to the ceiling, and the largest symbol of all began to glow.

"You'll have to help with the last bit," he said with a grin, indicating the star on his shirt. Shannon lifted her hand towards it, and the centre began to spin. The same shimmer as before rose up from the spellstation and gradually surrounded them. Shannon closed her eyes.

6 The Course Is Set

A moment later, Jax said softly, "I don't believe it!" and Shannon very nervously opened her eyes again.

To begin with, Shannon didn't trust what she was seeing. "I'm not sure I believe it either," she whispered to Jax. For they were back in Shannon's garden, and she could hear the voices of her mother and sister fading away as they departed on their bike ride. Everything was exactly the same as when Jax had first arrived earlier that day. In fact, it appeared as if it actually was earlier that day, all over again.

Shannon frowned. "What happened to the other version of me?" she wondered. "I mean, at this exact moment, I was over there, by the tree."

"There is no other version of you," said Jax, shaking his head. "Everything is reset as we travel through the portal."

"What do you mean, the other me just

disappeared?" asked Shannon, shivering a little. "That's a bit freaky."

"No, it's not exactly that," Jax tried again. "There can only be one version of you. At the time we projected the spell and walked through the portal, this now becomes real."

"So you could actually rewrite history?" enquired Shannon.

"Not really," Jax replied. "The portal memory only lasts a few hours, so you couldn't go back further than that. The portals are made that way so that a harvesting trip could be redone if necessary."

Then he looked uncomfortable, and Shannon realised what he was saying.

"So that if you were seen by someone like me, you could go back and prevent it from happening?" she suggested. "Why didn't you do that last time then?"

"Well, your Sygnus key needs to be activated to access the portal memory. So I would have had to get an older magician to do it. I wasn't able to reactivate my own until today. As I told you earlier, it took a lot of magic.

"If I had told an older magician, it means the Council would have got to hear about it. And all this… us, today… it would never have happened."

He looked serious for a moment. "I don't

regret my decision."

Shannon didn't disagree with him. Despite being scared about the Code and the Council, she couldn't imagine going back now. It was frightening, but pretty exciting as well.

They looked at each other, and Shannon grinned. "This day is just incomprehensible," she managed, shaking her head. She walked to the garden table and picked up the bottle of water she had been drinking with her lunch.

She was surprised to find that it was still slightly cold. But of course, she thought, it's only been outside for half an hour at most. She took a long drink, then turned back to Jax, offering him the bottle. He took it from her gladly, and quickly finished the rest of the water.

"What now?" asked Shannon.

"Well," Jax began, "even though it's been, as you say, an incomprehensible day, we unfortunately haven't answered any of our original questions."

"I know a lot more than I did earlier," argued Shannon.

"Yes," allowed Jax, "but in terms of why this is happening, and what the consequences might be, we know nothing."

He hesitated, before asking, "Will you come back with me? Later tonight? Now that we know the portal memory spell works, we could try again, knowing we have more time."

Shannon thought for a moment. "Yes, alright," she replied. Despite the tiredness sweeping over her from another trip through the portal so soon, she agreed with Jax. There was no way they could stop now.

They decided Jax would return at midnight. He was determined to spend the next few hours on Androva coming up with a plan. He advised Shannon to rest as much as possible.

"I can give you a Portal Remedy when you return with me," he said, "but you will feel the after-effects of this latest trip for several hours before you start to feel better."

He turned to go, then hesitated.

"What is it?" asked Shannon.

"I have to tell you…" he began, looking nervous.

"What?" repeated Shannon.

"One week ago, that was not the first time I have been here, to your garden. It was not the first time I have seen *you*."

Shannon smiled. "I know that," she replied.

Jax was surprised. "How?" he asked.

"I heard you say 'I've never been caught before,' and the more I thought about it, the more I realised that you must have taken this kind of risk already. I don't know when or how you did it, because I've never seen you before that day. But someone fearless like you... it makes perfect sense," she finished.

Jax looked very relieved that Shannon was taking the news so calmly. Then he smirked a little. "Fearless, huh?" he repeated.

"That's not necessarily a compliment," Shannon continued, raising her voice slightly. "I could just as easily have said arrogant, or stupid. Being fearless isn't always a good thing! And I *definitely* didn't say that I was happy you'd spied on me without me knowing."

Jax looked shamefaced. "I only saw you once before," he corrected. "And I wasn't spying. I had to check that it was safe to go ahead with the harvest, because a light was shining in your room."

Shannon was actually quite reassured to hear his explanation, though she tried not to show it. She hadn't liked the idea that Jax might have been spying on her many times. "I must have been reading," she told him. "That's the only reason my light would have been on late at night."

"You were," Jax confirmed. "You did not notice me at all. I was kind of annoyed about that. I mean, I was glad that I wasn't breaking the Code, but I couldn't believe that a book was more engaging than me!" Then he stopped, embarrassed at how conceited he sounded.

"Imagine that…" started Shannon, in a mock-horrified voice. "A mere book was more interesting than the amazing Jax, the greatest underage magician the world has ever seen!"

Reluctantly, Jax joined in her laughter. "But seriously," he said, "what was it about? I have never in my life been as transfixed as you were by a simple book."

"I don't know which book it was," replied Shannon. "I have lots and lots of them. I love reading. Well, at least I love reading fiction."

"Fiction?" repeated Jax.

"Yes," said Shannon, tiredness making her a bit impatient. "You know, stories, made-up tales about anything and everything. But especially stories that take place in imaginary worlds, and that contain, well, magic."

"I don't really understand," said Jax, puzzled. "I only know of books that contain the facts about magic and history. Fabrications and falsehoods are surely not to be encouraged, and certainly not to be written down."

"I'm too tired to explain," Shannon said wearily. Then she had an idea. One of her books was on the garden table from when she had been reading earlier, at the time her parents called her to lunch. She offered it to Jax and suggested he take it with him.

Then she said, "If I don't go and rest soon, I

think I might actually fall over."

Jax hastily apologised. "Until later then?" he confirmed, and Shannon nodded decisively. He turned to leave, and this time Shannon could see the hazy shimmer of the portal as he stepped into it and disappeared.

She went back into the house and slowly climbed the stairs to her room. She could hear that the football match her father had intended to watch was only just starting, so she knew she would be undisturbed for a while. Collapsing onto her bed, she fell asleep almost immediately.

Jax arrived back on Androva and returned quickly to his room. He wanted to be alone to think for a while. Despite his outwardly confident appearance, he was actually feeling quite shaken about the events of the afternoon.

All his life so far had been governed by the rules of the Code, and as an extension of that, his father's expectations. Now he felt as if everything he believed in was being turned on its head.

It was one thing to take risks and joke about testing the rules, but the reality of the after-effects was taking some getting used to. It would be wrong to say that Jax did not care about the implications of what he was doing, or about his father's good opinion. He was not a malicious boy. Now that he was alone, his confidence wavered a little.

He decided to open Shannon's book. He hoped that if he distracted himself for a while, it might be easier to see things more clearly when he returned to the problem. He was quickly drawn into the story, and read several chapters one after the other, before lifting his head and realising that sundown was almost upon Androva.

He was astonished at how entertained he was by the book. It did not seem to matter that a part of him knew it was all made up. There was a larger part of him that was only too happy to believe in the imaginary world created by the author.

Immediately he made a decision. He would go forwards, and continue to investigate the strange events that had taken place since his first meeting with Shannon. Surely if he put his mind to it, he could be as brave and resourceful as the hero in the storybook. Happy to have made his mind up, he was just about to return for one more chapter, when there was a loud knock at his door.

He jumped slightly at the sudden noise. His first reaction was to hide the book, which he quickly concealed behind one of the heavy green-and-gold curtains. He then hurried to open the door, expecting that it would be his father, and not wanting to raise suspicion by keeping him waiting.

It was indeed Revus, but he was accompanied by another Council member, Marcus. Jax was not happy to see Marcus, though he kept his face from showing it.

Marcus was a man of similar age to Revus, but shorter and thinner, with wispy brown hair and rather watery blue eyes. His appearance was unimpressive, but he was a magician of great power, and had an almost fanatical devotion to his job.

He and Jax had met several times in less than positive circumstances, most recently after Jax's daylight trip to Terra one week before. Marcus had called for Jax to be punished after this wrongdoing, and he had been angry that Revus had only given him a telling-off. Jax was a little afraid of Marcus, but was very determined not to let Marcus know it.

The two men entered the room, and Jax moved backwards to sit on the window seat again. Marcus looked around the room with a rather disdainful look on his face, pausing when he noticed the ceiling and the colourful mists swirling there. "You give the boy far too much freedom, Revus," he declared. "He is a danger to everything, with his disrespect for the Code and his experimenting."

Revus sighed. He knew Marcus was correct, but he still hoped that Jax would conform of his own accord without him having to impose the punishment that Marcus wanted.

There was also the matter of the harvest quota. Jax was the single best magic-taker on Androva, and they could not afford to lose him, especially now.

"We need to speak to you, Jax," began Revus, his expression even more solemn than usual. "You must increase the quantity of your trips to Terra in the next two nights. The quota... there is a problem with some of the other harvests."

Jax was surprised. This was a significant confession for the Council to make. The quota was part of Androvan life, always protected, always secure. "Of course," he replied. "I will do whatever the Council requires."

Marcus suddenly stepped forwards, staring into Jax's face with an intensity that would have made Jax move backwards, had he not already been seated with his shoulders against the window.

"You will indeed do whatever we require," he said menacingly. "You will follow the rules of the Code, and you will accept the consequences if you do not." Jax turned his gaze towards his father.

"Oh yes," Marcus continued with a small, rather nasty smile. "Your father accepts that the time for tolerance is past. I will be watching you *very* closely from now on." He turned and left the room without waiting for Revus to follow him.

Revus walked to Jax and sat across from him, looking into the green eyes that so reminded him of Jax's mother. He sighed again.

"I cannot express how important it is that you follow the rules in future," he said seriously.

Close up, Jax noticed that his father looked very tired. "Is everything alright, Father?" he asked awkwardly. "Are you alright?"

Revus closed his eyes for a moment. "All will be well," he responded. "When we return the quota to its required level, things will get back to normal." Jax nodded, not entirely convinced, but knowing it was pointless to ask his father for any more details.

He was well aware that Revus would never reveal any forbidden information to an underage magician. Even if that underage magician was his own son.

"Promise me that you will not give Marcus cause to punish you," continued Revus. "I need to know that you understand the seriousness of your position."

"I understand," responded Jax. "Believe me, Father, I do. I will make the extra trips and harvest as much magic as I can obtain."

Revus got up and made his way to the door. "You will start tonight," he confirmed as he left the room. "There is no time to waste."

Jax watched Revus leave. He had not made the promise that his father had requested.

7 Reinforcements

Jax wondered if his father had noticed that he had not made the promise that was asked of him. He knew he was about to embark on a course of action that would not only give Marcus cause to punish him, but could incur the wrath of the entire Council. But something was going on.

If there was a problem with the harvest quota, he had to try to find out what was causing it. Especially if he was the one who had triggered the problem in the first place, he thought guiltily.

He resolved to have an early dinner, with the aim of making the required additional harvesting trip with Darius as soon as possible that night. He had no way of getting any message to Shannon, so he intended to do everything possible to keep their midnight appointment.

Shannon, meanwhile, had woken from her sleep feeling almost completely back to normal. She ate dinner with her parents and sister, making an effort to behave as she usually did and join in the conversation.

She concentrated very carefully on suppressing the magic force field inside her head, finding after a few minutes that it was quite straightforward to push it into a corner of her mind and ignore it. She certainly didn't want her hands to start glowing at the dinner table!

After helping to clear away the meal, she returned to her room, saying she wanted to read before getting an early night. As she often spent Sunday evening in her room reading, this did not surprise her parents, and she was left in peace.

Once back in her room, she paced up and down, free at last to think about her afternoon with Jax and what had happened to her. She quickly realised that there was no chance she would be able to come up with any answers on her own, so she decided to spend some time finding out what her magic was capable of.

She remembered Jax saying that on her world things were easy for magicians because of all the living magic everywhere. But, she reasoned to herself, Jax had harvested most of the nearby magic from her garden just a week ago, so maybe she would not find it so easy.

She stopped pacing and turned to face the window. Then, closing her eyes, she focused on the force field inside her head, extending it until she could feel it in her hands again. It happened very fast, and the glow given off by her hands was quite luminous.

"Up," she said softly, keeping her eyes open. Immediately she rose into the air, finding that she had to push one hand against the ceiling to stop herself from hitting it. This was partly because the height of her ceiling was so much lower than Jax's had been, but also because it happened much faster this time.

Experimenting, she soon found she could go in any direction, up, down, left, right, just by focusing on where she wanted to be. She also discovered that she did not need to speak any words, not even inside her head. "Well, this is pretty cool," she said to herself, finally coming to a stop next to her wardrobe. "What can I try next?"

Suddenly her mobile phone beeped with a text. It was Penny. She wanted to know what Shannon had been up to all day. At once Shannon felt guilty, as she had really not given Penny a second thought. She texted back something vague about family commitments, promising to call for Penny at the usual time the following morning on the way to school.

Then she switched off her phone. She felt uneasy about misleading her friend, but couldn't see any way to tell Penny the truth about what was happening. How could she explain that she was now a magician with glowing hands who could fly through the air? Penny would think she had totally lost it.

Shannon lay back on the bed, seeing from her alarm clock that she still had three hours to wait until Jax would arrive. I can't just sit here worrying about it, she thought. Who knows what will happen later tonight? I might as well have some fun with this whole magic thing while I can.

And so she did. She decided to try to use the magic glow from her hands to tidy her room. After a few false starts, she was able to move her clothes from the floor and the chair to the wardrobe.

It wasn't quite as impressive as when Mary Poppins had tidied the children's nursery in the film, but Shannon was pretty pleased. After all, it was a lot more fun than picking it all up herself. And once the wardrobe door was shut again you couldn't see the mess inside. Gaining confidence, she started on her books.

Shannon had a lot of books, and several bookshelves on the wall opposite her bed. Gradually, she surrounded all the books dotted around the room with the silver glow. Then she pushed her hands towards the bookshelves, and the books obediently rushed towards them. One after another, they lined themselves up, until there were only two books left.

There was not quite room for these last two books, something that Shannon hadn't realised because she had never tidied them all away before. She watched as the two books forced their way onto the shelf, causing two different books at the end to fall onto the floor. The fallen books flew back up and attacked the books that had taken their place, snapping their covers like angry paper crocodiles.

At first Shannon giggled at the sight, but then she realised how noisy it was becoming. She tried to grab the books and carry them across to her bedside table, but they kept trying to return to the shelves. Shannon began to panic, not knowing what to do, until she realised that she had to drop the spell. As soon as she figured this out, the books returned to normal.

Relieved, she decided not to push her luck with any more experimenting. She changed into her favourite purple T-shirt, hoping that it might bring her some good luck. Then she redid the varnish on her fingernails in a brighter purple, with tiny rainbows in the corners of her thumbnails.

When she checked the clock again it was ten minutes to midnight. She hastily went into the bathroom and cleaned her teeth, before tiptoeing down the stairs and carefully opening the door to the garden.

All was dark and still under the chestnut tree. Shannon considered magnifying the glow on her hands so that she could see a bit better, but decided against it for fear that she would be noticed from the house. Where was he? Surely it was past midnight by now?

She leaned against the tree, looking back up at the house to make sure there were no signs that anyone was awake in her parents' bedroom.

"Miss me?" whispered a familiar voice in her ear. Shannon, taken by surprise, spun round to see the mischievous grin of her partner in crime.

"Yes, I've done nothing but count the hours before I could see you again. I don't know how I survived," she said with a straight face.

"Understandable." He nodded, playing along. "I am the greatest underage magician the world has ever seen, after all."

They grinned at each other, actually very happy to be starting the next part of their adventure together. Jax took Shannon's hand, and they stepped into the portal.

Shannon found it easier this time, perhaps because the garden was now as dark as the portal room. There was not the same shocking contrast between the sunlight and the darkness as she had found before. Then she looked up in surprise to see someone else in the portal room waiting for them. She recognised Darius immediately.

"You must be Shannon," he said with a shy smile.

"And you must be Darius," Shannon replied.

Then she turned to Jax with a questioning look. "Reinforcements," he replied. "We can trust Darius, and after what happened this evening, we need all the help we can get."

"What happened this evening?" asked Shannon.

"I will tell you in a moment," responded Jax. "First we have to get to a safer room, and then you need to take a Portal Remedy."

Darius opened the door to check the coast was clear, and then they made their way along the corridor and up the winding staircase. This time Jax took a different route through the house, and they ended up in a large, slightly dusty hall.

It had hardly any furniture and very high ceilings, and the floor and walls were plain. Jax immediately fetched a small blue glass from one of the alcoves and poured out a clear liquid from the bottle that was alongside it. Shannon didn't hesitate to drink the remedy this time. Then she turned expectantly to Jax.

"I don't really know where to begin," he said. "There is something going on, and it doesn't make any sense at the moment."

He told Shannon about the visit from his

father at the start of the evening, leaving out the part about Marcus. Then he told her about the harvesting trip that he and Darius had made afterwards.

"It was like we had gone back too soon to the same location," Jax explained. "The living magic just wasn't as powerful as usual. We even made a second trip to somewhere different, but it was the same.

"My father told me earlier that there was a problem with the harvest quota, and tonight I saw it for myself. Even using all our skills, Darius and I could only collect half as much as we usually do."

"According to my father, other magic-takers are not even managing half," added Darius in a quiet voice.

"Your father?" Shannon asked.

"He works in the Repository of Magic," replied Darius. "He performs maintenance and the daily count of harvest receipts in the east section. The new harvests have never been so low.

"My father is not permitted to discuss the grand total of the daily count, so I don't know for sure, but I think that we are in danger of missing the harvest quota for the month, which has never happened before."

Shannon remembered the third rule of the

Code: "*The Council shall enforce all necessary measures to collect the harvest quota in full, each month without fail*." It didn't sound like missing the quota was an option, even if it was by a small margin.

"I should be making a third harvesting trip with Darius right about now," admitted Jax. "But I couldn't break our agreement."

"Will they send more magicians?" Shannon asked. "Surely some of the older more powerful magicians would be able to harvest more magic than you two. No offence," she added hastily.

Jax grinned. "None taken," he responded. "The thing is that underage magicians are the best magic-takers." He stopped, before continuing in a more sarcastic tone. "It's because of our amazingly brilliant unspoiled potential or something."

"What my friend is trying to say," interrupted Darius with an exasperated look at Jax, "is that the coming of age ceremony fixes your magic ability forever. After that point it's very difficult to collect additional magic and travel back with it because you can't hold any more than your fixed ability will allow. You can use the living magic to enhance your ability at a particular moment, but you can't harvest it."

"That actually makes sense," said Shannon thoughtfully. "It must be very frustrating for the older magicians though. No wonder they have such a strict set of rules. How could they control you otherwise?"

Jax and Darius looked at each other. "Darius thinks the rules should be followed," said Jax. "Whereas I think they might be due for re-evaluation."

"I don't necessarily disagree with you," protested Darius. "But I don't think this is the right way to prove it!" Then he looked at Shannon, before lowering his dark blue eyes, a bit embarrassed by his outburst.

"Part of me finds this as exciting as Jax does. What he has told me... about your bravery, about your magic abilities, and about the storybook you lent him—it's amazing." Shannon blushed at hearing these compliments. She looked at Jax, and he blushed a little too.

Darius continued. "But I can't believe that this is not connected to the problems Androva is having with the harvest quota. The timing is too coincidental for them not to be linked."

There was silence for a moment as all three considered this. Shannon was the first to speak, and she turned to Darius. "One week ago, you were the one who said there would be consequences if I opened my eyes. And I did open them. I'm sorry," she said sincerely, and he nodded.

Then he murmured, "Thank you, but we are all to blame for this."

She continued. "I only travelled here to find out what these consequences were, so that I could try to prevent them. Do you think they are already happening? Is it too late?"

8 The Plan

There was another silence after Shannon had finished talking. It went on for some time, no one being willing to admit they were afraid that the answer to her final question was Yes. Finally Jax started to speak.

"Let's not spend any more time and energy on something we just don't know the answer to yet," he suggested. "We should talk about the plan now that Shannon is here," he went on, looking at Darius. "Then we might be able to figure out how serious this is, and if it's fixable." Darius nodded his agreement.

"What *is* the plan then?" asked Shannon.

"Well, the biggest problem we have is lack of information. "Darius and I are underage, so we don't know anything about the treaty, or the consequences of not meeting the quota, or breaking the Code and all that stuff," replied Jax. "So I thought we should just go ahead and find out," he concluded, looking pleased with himself.

Shannon was sceptical. "Is there a spell you can project to make yourself immediately four years older then?" she said. "Or do you now have the ability to fast-forward time?"

"Very funny," Jax responded. "And no, that's not quite what I had in mind."

"Jax had the idea that we could break into the restricted section in the Repository of Records," Darius explained.

Seeing that Shannon didn't understand, he continued. "The Repository of Records is where all the books of spells and historic accounts are kept. It has a restricted section that you can only access when you are of age. Entry is dependent on your Sygnus key being activated. We are pretty sure that we will find information about the treaty and everything else in the restricted section."

Shannon understood. "And Jax can use his Sygnus to gain access!" she said excitedly. "Just like he did when he travelled alone through the portal earlier!"

She noticed that Darius had not lost his serious expression. "What's the matter?" she asked him. "It sounds like a great plan."

"It's not quite as simple as that," replied Darius. "The restricted section is guarded as well. The Council doesn't believe in taking any chances."

"There must be a way," said Shannon. "Why would you say you have a plan, if it's impossible to carry out?"

Jax and Darius exchanged glances again. "Well?" Shannon prompted.

"We can, in theory, get past the custodian," said Jax. "But it will require the use of an Unauthorised Spell."

"OK," said Shannon. "I guess that's not great, but it's not like we haven't broken other rules already anyway."

"Yes, exactly," agreed Jax. "So it's a bit late to start worrying about that now, right?"

"No!" said Darius firmly. "You have to tell her everything, Jax," he insisted.

Jax faced Shannon, who looked back at him slightly nervously. "Alright," he started. "I'll tell you. We will have to use a Deceiving Spell if we are to stand any chance of success. Aside from fighting our way in, which I disregarded because someone would surely hear us, there is no other tactic that is likely to succeed."

"OK," replied Shannon. "That sounds reasonable."

"There is more," continued Jax. "We only know of one previous occasion where a Deceiving Spell has been used on a government official. And the reason we know about it is because the magician who used the spell was caught. His punishment was to suffer the Spell of Removal."

Shannon gulped. Now she understood why Darius was so concerned. But Jax hadn't finished yet.

"Darius and I cannot reach agreement about which of us is to project the spell," he said. "I think it should be me. I have been the instigator of everything that has happened up to now, so what's one more broken rule? But Darius thinks it should be him because he has some crazy idea that I need protecting." As he said this, he rolled his eyes to demonstrate how ridiculous he found it.

"I'm your *friend*," countered Darius, raising his voice. "We're a *team*! I agreed to the daylight trip to Terra one week ago, and I accept responsibility for the outcome. You have to let me play my part. At least this way, if we are caught, there is a chance we can both avoid the Spell of Removal. If you are the one who projects the Deceiving Spell, on top of everything else you have done, there will be no way to stop it," he finished more quietly.

Shannon looked at the two boys. She could see things from both sides. Then all of a sudden she knew what to do. "I'll project the spell," she declared. Jax and Darius turned to her, both of them already starting to protest. "It's the only logical thing to do," she said, speaking over their objections. "Then you will be safe from any punishment. At least, you will be safe from any punishment related to the Deceiving Spell."

"But what about you?" asked Darius, looking worried. "If we are caught, you are likely to be caught with us, and once the Council are involved, we cannot protect you."

"I know that," replied Shannon, sounding a lot more confident than she felt. Her stomach was actually doing somersaults with fear. "But I don't even come from Androva, so maybe I can't be punished in the same way. It's the best option, you know it is."

Jax and Darius reluctantly agreed. Jax thought back to the warning he had received from Marcus, feeling quite uneasy despite his determination not to let it bother him. He decided that the best thing to do was to make very sure that they weren't caught.

He glanced at Shannon, whose brown eyes were steady as she returned his gaze. Jax was impressed again by how brave she was being, and he determined that he would not fail his new friend.

"OK then, let's start the lesson," he said firmly.

"The lesson?" enquired Shannon.

"Yes, not only do we have to teach you how to project the spell, you also need to learn some basic attack and defence spells. You know, in case of emergencies," he added.

Then he grinned, his natural mischievousness returning. "Anyway, Darius here could do with a training session against someone he might actually be able to beat for a change!"

Shannon laughed as Darius pretended to be offended. Then the two boys, taking it in turns to speak, explained that the hall they were standing in was actually used as a training room. It was covered by a Protection Spell.

This prevented any permanent injury arising from spells that were projected within it. Darius pointed out the very faint blue haze that hovered in front of the walls, floor, and ceiling. This was the evidence that the Protection Spell was in place, and Shannon could see it quite clearly once she knew what to look for.

Jax started by describing the Deceiving Spell that he wanted to use. It had three layers to it. The first was invisibility, to make sure that they could not be seen. The second was silence, to make sure that any sounds they made would not be heard. The final layer was distraction.

This was the trickiest part of the spell. It would cause the custodian to be looking in a different direction when they were entering the restricted section.

As Jax said, there was not much point being silent and invisible if the custodian noticed that the door he or she was guarding was opening of its own accord!

They had some fun practicing the three spells, and Shannon was pleased that it didn't take her too long to learn how to use them. The final proof that she had mastered all three layers was when she was able to creep up undetected behind Jax and flick his ear.

"Hey!" he cried—not hurt, but slightly annoyed that Shannon had managed to fool him so easily. (Which is a bit silly when you think about it. After all, the success of their plan now depended on Shannon's ability to master the spell).

Then Jax described the three basic Combat Spells that could be used to incapacitate another magician. He added that all magicians were taught them. However, the use of them was only authorised in a very few situations. The spells were as follows:

1. The Containment Spell

A circular band of concentrated magical energy is projected by the attacking magician. It disappears inside the other magician's head to restrict the source of the force field. Resisting makes it very painful. The only way out is to suppress the force field to get around the band. It is a test of nerve as much as skill.

2. The Scattering Spell

This spell causes the defending magician's magic to disperse in all directions within their body, as if a magical bomb has been detonated. They should concentrate on their original spark, and use this as a magnet for their magic until they have accumulated enough of it to fight back.

3. The Spell of Immobility

This spell causes all the magic in the defending magician's body to be suspended, as if it were frozen in time. It is a very difficult spell to project and maintain effectively, and most attacking magicians are only able to slow down the magic of their opponent, rather than bring it to a complete stop. There is no defence, but eventually the spell will fail due to the strength that is required to project it.

By the time Jax had finished all these descriptions, Shannon was looking a bit overwhelmed. "The Containment Spell is the most important," he added, "because it's the one that any government official is most likely to use on you.

"OK," he said decisively. "The best way for you to really learn all of this is to experience it for yourself." Then he turned, and before Shannon realised what was happening, his hands had projected a band of silver light which immediately wrapped itself around Darius's head. Instantly, the band seemed to tighten and disappear into his hair. It had taken no more than a couple of seconds.

Darius staggered to the side, and Shannon could see the pain on his face, before he drew himself upright again. She made to reach out to him, trying to help, but Jax shook his head.

The boys stood for a minute or two, engaged in a silent battle as Jax tried to keep the containment band in place, and Darius tried to escape it. Eventually Darius started laughing, and Shannon realised that he had escaped the band.

"Not bad," said Jax reluctantly, and Darius, still laughing, replied, "Not bad yourself!"

Shannon was half shocked, half intrigued by what she had seen. She had imagined that fighting with magic would be all fireworks and broken furniture, but apparently it was more like a battle of wills. The magician who lost their nerve would lose the fight.

Jax turned to Shannon, raising his eyebrows. "Ready to try it yourself?" he asked.

She took a deep breath. "Yes," she replied firmly.

9 The Treaty

"Darius, you go first," said Jax. "I know you'll go easy on her, which is better to start with." Darius accepted the truth of what Jax was saying. He wouldn't feel right using his full strength against a brand-new untrained magician. The first couple of times, Darius was almost gentle, giving Shannon the chance to get used to the feel of the band inside her head. Then he started increasing the pressure, and she began to struggle to escape it.

"OK, enough," interrupted Jax, when Darius was about to project his Containment Spell for the fifth time. "We need to go faster. My turn." And with that, he pushed a band of silver light so quickly into Shannon's head that she shrank backwards.

It felt icy cold compared to the bands that Darius had created and extremely inflexible. Panicking, she pushed against it with all her strength and flinched as it started to really hurt. Looking across at Jax, she felt her eyes start to fill with tears from the pain.

His green eyes were kind, but the band inside her head did not let up. "No," he said gently, "don't fight it. You have to suppress your magic in order to escape it." Shannon concentrated. She imagined that she was back at home at the dinner table, hiding her magic away so that her family would not see it. She felt it become smaller and smaller.

At first the band in her head kept pace with it, becoming smaller too, but eventually she could outrun it and she was free from the band. She took a shaky breath, able to smile at last. "Well done," said Jax.

They tried a few more times, until Shannon was almost enjoying it. It was like a game of mental hide-and-seek, as she tried to find different places to conceal her magic from the band that was trying to capture it. By the end, Jax was becoming fascinated by the methods she used to escape the spell. "You're a very fast learner," he told her. "I'm actually a bit envious."

"That's praise indeed," Darius was quick to point out.

Finally, aware that more than an hour had passed, Jax decided they just had time to practice the other two spells of attack. He encouraged

Shannon to defend herself by trying to project the spells back onto him and Darius.

He reasoned that she should experience being the attacker as well as the defender. Just in case there was ever a situation where she would need to fight back. He did not realise at the time just how important this final part of the lesson would prove to be.

At last they were ready. Before they left the hall, Shannon stopped the two boys. "This has been the most amazing day and night of my life," she said. "Whatever happens next, I am really glad I met you both."

"Me too," agreed Darius.

Jax didn't speak, but he squeezed her hand. Then, to lighten the mood, he pretended to be insulted, saying, "How dare you? I resent the suggestion that my plan might not be completely successful!"

Shannon smiled. "*Our* plan," she corrected.

The three friends found that it was still quiet as they walked back into the corridor. Jax led the way through his house, eventually arriving at a single side door which opened to the outside. It was fortunately a warm night, and the stars were shining brightly enough for the pathway to the road to be seen quite clearly. Shannon looked up. "These stars are amazing," she said in a low voice.

"Yes, they are much closer than the Terran stars," agreed Jax quietly. He pointed to the road, and they walked silently towards it. There were a lot of buildings up ahead, and within a little more than ten minutes they were among them.

She guessed that this was the capital Landor that Jax had told her about earlier. It was hard to tell in the half-light, but the buildings all seemed to be of a similar height, and were quite well spaced out.

They encountered no one else as they continued walking. It was certainly nothing like London, with its metal skyscrapers and twenty-four-hour noise. Eventually Jax drew her and Darius into a small side street. "Now," he instructed. Shannon concentrated for a moment, then projected the Deceiving Spell, one layer at a time.

Back on the main road, Jax pointed to a taller building up ahead, which was giving off a slightly greenish glow compared to the darkness of its neighbours. According to a small sign hanging above the entrance archway, this was the Repository of Records. There was still no one to be seen, and they entered quickly.

The glow that had been visible from the outside was stronger, as it was radiating from every surface. Jax had forewarned Shannon that this was due to the protective spells buried in the walls, floor, and ceiling, which were designed to prevent any theft of the records within.

She looked around curiously, finding that the building was a strange mixture of the old-fashioned and the new. The walls had been built out of smooth rock, and the doorways were all made from intricately carved wood. But the floor was luxuriously carpeted, and there was some kind of reception desk that looked just like you might find in a library on her world.

Jax and Darius moved forward, with Shannon following. They headed for a stairway at the end of the entrance corridor, and began to climb. It was just like the stairs leading from the portal room in Jax's house. Finally they reached the top floor, where the green glow appeared to be even stronger. There was only one door, and carved into it were the words "Restricted Section."

They paused, knowing it was time to see if their plan would work. Shannon concentrated with all her strength on the three layers of the spell she was making, and Jax pushed open the door.

They entered a small well-lit room, which contained a wooden desk and chair next to another doorway. A young man was seated at the desk, writing in a book. He did not look up as they entered.

Shannon was surprised that the custodian was

so ordinary-looking, but Jax and Darius knew very well that appearances on Androva were no indication of magical ability. This ordinary young man could be incredibly powerful. There was no way to tell just by looking at him.

Jax quickly walked towards the other doorway and attempted to activate his Sygnus. He did not dare to ask Shannon to do it this time, as she needed to use all her power for the Deceiving Spell. Darius moved forward to help Jax, and eventually his Sygnus started to spin.

The door did nothing at first, and then it slowly and silently opened. Jax and Darius immediately turned to Shannon and beckoned her forward, then all three walked through. The door shut behind them with a decisive click.

Shannon sighed with relief at being able to lift the Deceiving Spell. Jax and Darius looked at her with something resembling awe. "You did it!" whispered Jax, slightly amazed at how well it had gone.

"We all did it," she whispered back, very relieved that she had not let them down.

Moving forwards, they found themselves in a large room with many bookshelves. Again, Shannon was surprised at how normal it all was, just like a library back home in fact. All the rows of shelves radiated outwards in a circle from a table in the centre.

This table was the most impressive item in the room. It was enormous, made of a rich brown wood, with the elaborate carving she had come to expect. In addition, it was embellished with lines of glowing silver patterns. As Shannon moved closer, she realised the patterns formed words, but she could not read them, as they were shifting and changing too quickly for her to identify the letters.

"We need to find the treaty," whispered Jax urgently. "As quickly as possible."

They each began to explore a different set of shelves, quickly becoming frustrated as they realised there was no obvious system to the types of books and the order in which they were arranged. Then Shannon had an idea.

She returned to the table in the centre of the room and looked again at the silver patterns. She held out her hands above the table and made them glow. I want to read you, she thought silently, projecting the glow from her hands down onto the table. Then again, with more intensity, she repeated the words.

As she watched, the shapes and letters began to form into sentences across the table from left to right. The first sentence began "We, the undersigned, do hereby agree…"

She realised at once that it was the treaty!

"Jax! Darius!" she whispered as loudly as she

dared.

"What is it? Are you OK?" replied Darius, rushing over to her, with Jax close behind him.

"It's the treaty!" she whispered excitedly. "It's *in* the table!"

Darius and Jax looked down and saw that she was right. They had been expecting the treaty to be engraved on an ancient parchment hidden deep inside the bookshelves, but in fact it was a living thing, made out of magic. Shannon had found it. Slightly fearfully, they began to read the silver words.

We, the undersigned, do hereby agree, as elected representatives of the worlds of Androva and Terra, to uphold the following treaty from now until eternity. We have joined together to defeat the Evil that threatens us all. As we require the magic and skills from both our worlds to achieve this, the following terms are finally agreed:

– Androva, being better able to regulate its use of magic and control its magicians, is charged with containing the Evil

– Terra, having plentiful living magic available in its woodlands, is charged with sacrificing this magic to supply Androva, whose magicians will harvest it in accordance with the quota

– Androva will add the following three rules to its Code, and abide by them absolutely

1. When travelling to Terra, each Androvan magician shall take all precautions necessary to ensure that his or her presence is unknown, unsuspected, and undetected by any Terran
2. No underage magician is permitted to travel to Terra unaccompanied
3. The Council shall enforce all necessary measures to collect the harvest quota in full, each month **without fail**

– Terra will allow every single one of its magicians to suffer the Spell of Removal, and henceforth there will be no magicians on Terra

– Future generations of Terrans will have no

awareness of the existence of the treaty, and will therefore be protected from the knowledge that their magic has been forever sacrificed

– Future generations of Androvan magicians will be granted knowledge of this treaty at the coming of age ceremony, and will honour the Terran sacrifice by keeping the harvest a secret from all Terrans

– Both sides accept that if any of the above terms are not followed, then the treaty is broken

– If the treaty breaks, each world is no longer required to keep to the terms, and each world understands that containing the Evil may then not be possible

Signed...

A very long list of signatures appeared in turn, one after the other, fading in and out, until finally it stopped.

There was complete silence as they realised the significance of what they had just read. Darius looked absolutely horrified, and Jax, his usual confidence having disappeared, was feeling sick at the realisation of what he had done. Shannon was torn between fear and amazement at what she had just learned about the history of her world.

"We can't fix this," started Darius, his face pale.

"It's all my fault," said Jax, head bowed. The others tried to reassure him that they were all involved. But Jax knew that if he hadn't taken the risk of making that daylight trip to Terra one week before, none of this would have happened.

"What exactly is the Evil?" asked Shannon. "We don't know how serious the situation is until we can answer that."

Jax and Darius looked at her without answering. As far as they were concerned, this was really bad. They had seen first-hand how Darius's father and Jax's father had behaved earlier that day. They knew it was very serious.

Then they heard the sound of the door opening.

10 Capture

Jax reacted first, grabbing Shannon and Darius by the arms and pulling them backwards towards the bookshelves. They ran deep into one of the sections, as far as they could go, not stopping until they reached the end. Staring anxiously at each other, hearts pounding with fear, they waited to hear who had come through the door.

There was no sound at first. Whoever had entered the room had done so with silent footsteps. Then there was an exclamation of discovery, and a man's voice could be heard calling "Dorian? Can you come in here for a moment?"

Apparently Dorian was the custodian who had been sitting outside. A short conversation then took place, but the voices were too quiet for Jax, Shannon, and Darius to hear what was being discussed. It was soon clear what had happened however.

The same man's voice was raised to say, "You might as well show yourself, I know there is someone in here. And I also know you are not permitted. I can recognise that the treaty has been read just a few moments ago, but Dorian tells me he has seen no one gain entry this night."

There was a pause, and then the voice continued, becoming angrier.

"Come now, this is a waste of my time and yours. I *will* find you, and you will not enjoy the methods I will use."

Jax had gone completely white. He recognised the voice as belonging to Marcus. For a few seconds he tried to think frantically of a way that they could escape, but almost straight away he realised it was impossible. He turned to Darius.

"It is Marcus," he said despairingly, in a low voice.

Darius looked alarmed. "Are you sure?" he whispered back.

"Yes, I am certain," replied Jax in the same defeated manner. Shannon was about to ask who Marcus was, but she hesitated. She had never seen Jax look like this before, as if all the fight had gone out of him.

"I am going to give myself up," continued Jax.

"No!" whispered Darius and Shannon at the same time.

"Yes, I am." He put his hand over his face for

a moment, trying to collect himself. "It has to be me. It can't be Darius, because Marcus will never believe Darius capable of doing such a thing on his own. He will just keep looking until he finds an accomplice. That means you will both be found as well. At least this way, there is a good chance you will both escape."

"But…" started Darius. "It's *Marcus*! You can't face him alone," he said desperately.

"This is becoming tiresome," Marcus called. "My patience is about to run out, and I really don't think you want that to happen, do you?"

Part of Jax was very scared, but another part of him was determined to go ahead. "I am to blame," he said. "I must try to make amends. And besides, I need you to take Shannon back to Terra. This is not her world. We must try to protect her from all this."

Darius was silent, unable to disagree with Jax. Though he could not bear the thought of his friend facing Marcus without help, he also knew he could not abandon Shannon.

"I'm so sorry," Darius began, but Jax cut him off, saying, "We're out of no time."

Then he smiled at Darius and Shannon with a hint of his old bravado. "Promise me you'll remember?" he asked. "Remember me as I am now? Before they…" At this, his voice trailed off, and he couldn't finish. Before they perform the

Spell of Removal, he thought. And then he walked away.

Shannon could hardly see, because her eyes were full of tears. How was this happening? Darius was trying to be brave, but she could feel him trembling beside her. They waited, not moving, until they heard the voice of Marcus again.

"Well, well, well," he began slowly. "I can't quite believe it." Then he gave an unpleasant laugh. "I have been waiting for this day for so long. I knew I would eventually catch you doing something inexcusable, but I never expected that you would make it quite so easy for me."

There was a pause. Shannon and Darius could see nothing of what was happening. They could only wait to hear what would happen next. There was no reply from Jax, and eventually Marcus spoke again.

"Nothing to say in your defence, boy?" he sneered. "You know what will happen—your father cannot protect you now. I intend to recommend an irreversible punishment. Are you not going to beg me for mercy?"

Finally Jax spoke. "I will not *beg* you for anything," he said quietly, in a voice that was shaking very slightly. Shannon's heart went out to him, and then she felt an anger against Marcus so powerful that she could hardly keep still. She became aware that Darius was frantically trying to cover her hands, which were glowing intensely.

Quickly she tried to calm down her anger, and the glow receded. But she was still filled with a cold fury towards Marcus, and was determined that one day she would get the chance to do something about it.

Marcus was talking again. "We will see how brave you are once the interrogation starts. I am very interested to find out exactly how you managed to accomplish this particular offence. I'm actually quite impressed. Do I need to use the Containment Spell, or are you going to come willingly?"

Shannon and Darius could not hear what Jax replied, but apparently Marcus was satisfied with the answer, because he then said, "Dorian! I will be taking this underage intruder to the Council examination rooms."

His voice became fainter, and they guessed he was walking out of the doorway. "Please go and inform Revus that I need to talk to him about his son on a matter of extreme importance. I intend to…" His voice became so indistinct they could no longer hear it.

They waited, wanting to be sure that Marcus and Dorian had both departed before leaving their hiding place. Eventually, they could not bear to delay any longer, and they walked towards the exit.

Though Shannon had a lot of questions she wanted to ask of Darius, she realised that the first thing they had to do was escape. Otherwise Jax's surrender would have been for nothing. At last they reached the main entrance on the ground floor again, and they were able to hurry past the empty desk to get back outside. They had only walked a short distance, with Darius setting quite a fast pace, when Shannon tugged at his arm and drew him into a side street.

"Who is Marcus?" she whispered urgently. Darius shook his head, saying that there was no time to discuss anything now, because they had to get back to the portal room straight away. But Shannon persisted. "You can't send me back without knowing who he is," she argued.

"OK," Darius agreed. "But we must be very quick. Marcus is a member of the Council. He works alongside Revus, who is Jax's father. He is a very powerful magician and specialises in the enforcement of the Code.

"He recommends any appropriate punishments to the rest of the Council, who then each cast their vote either in favour of the recommended punishment or against it. Marcus executes the punishment there and then so the Council may observe that it is correctly done."

Shannon took a moment to consider this

information. Then she asked, "So what's the deal between Marcus and Jax? They obviously know each other."

"Yes." Darius nodded. "Jax has come to the attention of the Council on a number of occasions. One week ago was the first time that any punishment has been recommended for him. This was after our daylight trip to Terra. But the Council voted against the punishment."

"What about you?" questioned Shannon. "You made the daylight trip as well."

"No punishment was recommended for me, as it was my first offence," admitted Darius. Then, looking uncomfortable, he continued. "And I didn't know at the time, but Jax took full responsibility, claiming he had tricked me into agreeing. I tried to take some of the blame, but I failed." He looked upset. "And I failed again tonight."

Shannon didn't know what to say. "There was nothing either of us could have done," she tried. But she also felt very bad about allowing Jax to surrender alone. They turned back to the road and continued on their way, soon arriving back at the house.

Darius led Shannon through the corridors and down the stairway to the portal room. After all these years as Jax's friend, he knew the way very well. All remained dark and quiet. Though Darius and Shannon were both fearful of being discovered and jumped at every small noise, they encountered no one.

"This is where I need your help," said Darius. "I have never travelled through a portal without another Androvan magician before. I know the series of symbols to use, but only when I have a partner."

"Maybe I should stay here then?" asked Shannon hopefully. She wasn't happy about the idea of returning home without knowing what had happened to Jax. Although she didn't want to remain stranded on Androva forever, she also didn't want to run back home like a coward. Not when her new friend had so bravely faced up to Marcus in order to save her and Darius.

"No," said Darius firmly. "Jax wanted me to take you back, so that is what I am going to do." He looked very determined. "I can at least do this one thing for him," he finished unhappily. "Even if I can't do anything else to help."

Shannon understood, and she decided not to argue with Darius. Even if she did convince him to let her stay on Androva, she had no plan for what to do next. It was very likely that they would just both be captured like Jax. "Alright," she answered. "How can I help you?"

"I think the best option is for me to teach you the order of the symbols, and you can activate them alongside me as if we were both underage Androvan magicians. I don't think the spellstation will care that you are actually a Terran magician. So it should work just as if I were travelling with Jax."

A shadow crossed his face as he realised he might never travel with Jax again.

"What about your Sygnus?" asked Shannon, looking at the silver image engraved on his black shirt. It was shaped like an arch, with zigzagging lines through the centre. "Maybe we could get it to start spinning, and then you won't need me at all."

"*No!*" responded Darius, almost shouting. Shannon took a step backwards, shocked.

"I have no intention of doing anything else that will go against the terms of the treaty or the Code," he explained in a quieter voice. Shannon immediately felt stupid for not thinking of that herself. She had been so worried about Jax that she had not remembered the treaty.

"Of course," she replied, going red. "I'm sorry, I should have thought of that. I'm an idiot."

Darius immediately calmed down when he saw how apologetic she was. "It's just that we still don't know exactly what this Evil is. I could tell from my father's comments about some of the other harvest trips earlier this evening that things were incredibly serious. I don't want to do anything to make it worse if I can help it."

"OK then," responded Shannon. "Show me what to do to activate the spellstation." Carefully she watched as Darius demonstrated the sequence of symbols that she had to illuminate, and then together they attempted to open the portal. On the second attempt, it worked. Stepping forward out of the shimmer that surrounded them, they were back in Shannon's garden, where it was still dark. Shannon turned to face Darius, unwilling to say goodbye, but knowing that Darius had to return to Androva.

"Thank you," she said with a very small smile. "And good luck…"

"The same to you," replied Darius. Then he turned back to the portal. He had just stepped into the shimmer, when he let out a small cry of shock. As Shannon watched, a shadowy figure grabbed him by both arms and dragged him forward. Then the shimmer abruptly disappeared.

11 The Prophecy

Shannon stepped forward, but she was too late. The portal had completely closed again. "No!" she cried, stamping her foot in frustration. Then she spun round to look up at her house, worried that somebody might have heard her. But everything remained quiet. She stood for a moment, infuriated that she was unable to do anything to help Darius. Who had grabbed him? Surely it wasn't Marcus?

He had mentioned taking Jax to the Council's examination rooms for interrogation. It seemed unlikely that he would have returned quickly enough to follow her and Darius back to the portal. Shannon tried not to think about what the interrogation would be like. Marcus had sounded as if he were going to enjoy it, which made her certain that Jax would not.

What now? Both her new friends were in trouble, and she was unable to think of anything that she could do to help them. After a few more moments of indecision, she decided to go back into the house and up to her room. She knew that she would soon start to feel very tired from travelling through the portal again. And this is exactly what happened. Despite her attempts to stay awake to figure out what to do next, she was soon fast asleep.

When Darius had been pulled back through the portal, he was afraid that he would find Marcus, or at the very least one of the Council's custodians, when he reached the other side. But he was shocked to see that it was Revus, Jax's father, who had grabbed him so forcefully.

Revus looked behind Darius expectantly as he stepped off the spellstation, and then said urgently, "Where is Jax? I need to speak to my son!"

"I…" Darius began, then stopped. What could he say? He couldn't tell Revus where Jax was. If Revus realised Darius had been involved in any of the events that had ended with Jax being taken for interrogation, then Darius would soon be taken for interrogation as well.

Now that Shannon was safely back on Terra, Darius did intend to give himself up sooner or later. He wanted to try to reduce Jax's punishment by sharing the blame with him. But he still hoped to find out a bit more about what was happening with the harvest quota first. So he did not answer Revus's question.

"Well?" Revus said impatiently when Darius paused. "I have had a message from the Council, and I need to speak to Jax to find out what is going on!"

"I don't know exactly where Jax is," started Darius. "We had a late training session after our last harvesting trip, and sometime after that we split up." Darius figured that this was all true, even if some of the more important details were missing.

"But you made another trip to Terra just now?" queried Revus. "What for?"

"Well, I…" Darius hesitated again, desperately trying to think of a plausible explanation that didn't involve actually lying. "I didn't go with Jax this time, I went with someone else. But Jax said we could use his spellstation. I didn't manage to harvest any magic though," he finished nervously, opening his hands so that Revus could see they were empty. He really hoped Revus would not ask where this other magician was.

Fortunately Revus was very preoccupied by the message that he had received from Dorian, and his thoughts immediately returned to his son.

"If you don't know where he is, then I will have to go to the Council offices," he muttered, and left the portal room. Darius sighed with relief. Waiting a little while to give Revus the chance to leave the house, he thought about what to do next.

Now that he had read the treaty, he understood a bit more about the importance of meeting the harvest quota. Surely magic-taking would take precedence over Jax's punishment? He and Jax had been the best harvesting team on Androva for the previous half-year. Perhaps the Council might be persuaded to at least delay any punishment until the quota was back to normal.

Darius tried not to think about the possibility that the quota might never get back to normal. Or about the Evil mentioned by the treaty. He decided that he would first try to find out for sure if the harvest quota was going to be missed. Then he could go to the Council and make his argument for a punishment delay. But more importantly, he would stand alongside his friend, and they would face it together.

Darius left the portal room, climbed the stairs, and walked quickly through the dark streets until he arrived at his own house. It was not as large and forbidding as Mabre House, but it was still a good size, with the same steep slate roof.

The walls were made from a warm yellow stone, however, and the interior was attractively furnished. Iona, Darius's mother, was fond of bright colours. Darius entered by a side door, not wanting to alert his parents to his arrival. He was hopeful he might be able to overhear something about the quota. He soon realised that the house was quiet though.

Disappointed, he decided to climb the stairs to his room and wait.

Walking along the downstairs hallway, he noticed a light coming through one of the doorways, where the door was slightly ajar. Curious, he moved towards it, making sure his footsteps were as quiet as possible. He peered through the crack and saw that his mother was seated inside.

Iona was a slender woman, with blonde hair like her son, and gentle features. Her talent for prophecy was known and respected throughout Androva. It was even said that Iona was sometimes consulted by the Council when they needed additional guidance on a matter of policy. Darius didn't know for sure if those rumours were true.

Prophecy was a skill that each underage magician had to study for at least one year. Few continued beyond this first year, as it was a difficult skill to master. Most had limited natural talent, including Darius. But he had always been fascinated by his mother's gift.

His earliest memories were of watching his mother create a Prophecy story for him at bedtime. The glow in her hands would magnify to create moving shapes, and she would tell him the story that she could see in the miniature world in front of her.

Moving closer to the door, Darius glimpsed the familiar glow of a Prophecy story. Iona was silent, concentrating on the shifting forms. Knowing that his mother hated to be interrupted when she was reading a prophecy, he was about to turn away and continue on to his room. But then he saw something that made him freeze in shock.

It was Shannon! At least, it was a small copy of Shannon, created by the Prophecy story. He moved to try to see more, but the position of the door did not allow it. He frowned in exasperation and was about to risk pushing the door further open, when he heard the sound of his father arriving home.

Quickly, he ran back towards the staircase and climbed to the top just in time to remain unseen. He heard his father calling, "Iona?" and his mother's soft reply. At first, the voices of his parents were muffled, so he tiptoed half-way back down the stairs until he was close enough to hear them better.

"I'm telling you, Marek, it's the same prophecy over and over," Iona said.

"It can't be," replied her husband. "It's not

possible. The fate of Androva cannot rest on the shoulders of a Terran girl."

Darius's eyes widened. What did his father mean?

"The fate of Androva remains uncertain, Marek," corrected Iona. "I can only see that without this girl, the future is sure to take a darker turn. And I do not say this lightly, because you know that our son and his friend are involved as well. I can't see how or when, but Darius and Jax are there."

"There are no Terrans in Androva's future," Marek replied more firmly. "People will think you are mad to suggest it. Your whole reputation will be affected if anyone hears about this. And right now Darius is upstairs in bed where he belongs because his last harvest trip was hours ago."

"I care little for my reputation when the stakes are this high," said Iona in a low voice. Then she asked, "What of the harvest quota? Did the night end well?"

For a moment, Marek did not answer, and Darius held his breath.

"No," he said heavily. "It did not end as we hoped. We have one more night to make up the shortfall."

"Then it is happening as I predicted," said Iona unhappily. "The Council will hold an Assembly tomorrow, and the girl may be here before sundown. What happens to her after that will decide our future."

"Alright, I can see that you are determined on this," sighed Marek. "Let me check on Darius, and you can show me the prophecy again. We will try to understand it together."

Darius heard his father's footsteps walking towards the door, and he immediately jumped up to run back upstairs. Heart pounding, he got into bed and pretended to be asleep. Soon after that he heard his door opening and he kept his eyes closed. After a few tense moments, the door closed again.

Darius continued to lay still, his thoughts all mixed up. He couldn't decide if his original idea of going to the Council to share the blame with Jax was still the right thing to do. His mother had said he was involved in the prophecy. But what did that mean? Should he try to bring Shannon back?

While Darius continued to battle with his thoughts, the first light of dawn was breaking over the Council offices. Jax did not notice, however, as he was so exhausted from his interrogation that he could barely hold his head up. Marcus was becoming increasingly frustrated, as Jax had refused to tell him anything.

No matter what threats, warnings, or spells Marcus used, Jax remained silent. Had Marcus thought about this, he would have realised that Jax had the makings of a very powerful magician. His resistance to the spells and his determination of spirit was a rare and impressive combination. But Marcus did not stop to notice, intent as he was on obtaining Jax's confession.

Of course, Marcus already had enough evidence to prove that Jax was guilty of a serious offence. Simply finding Jax in the restricted section, with the words of the treaty having been recently read, was enough. Marcus had informed Revus, and for the first time Revus had no words to offer in defence of his son.

But Marcus wanted more: he wanted Jax to admit that he had read the treaty and deceived the custodian. He was also desperate to learn exactly how Jax had managed to get into the restricted section. An underage magician using a spell that required a Sygnus key? It shouldn't have been possible. And finally, Marcus did not want to admit to the Council that the boy had resisted his interrogation. So he did not give up his attack.

Then something occurred to Marcus. "Perhaps I am approaching this in the wrong way…" he mused.

Jax was slumped in a plain wooden chair with his eyes half closed. The interrogation room was completely bare, with one small window high up in the far wall. It looked a lot like a prison cell. Jax paid no attention to Marcus as the older magician paced back and forth a couple of times. Then Marcus spoke again.

"I seem to remember that your friend—Darius is it?—was very keen to take some of the blame when you made your little daylight trip to Terra recently. I wonder if he might be of assistance to me now?"

As Marcus watched him, Jax was unable to prevent a flicker of panic from crossing his face. He knew that Darius would not withstand the interrogation as well as he had. Marcus's eyes gleamed. "I thought so," he said, with one of his nasty smiles. "I always win, boy, *always*. You would do well to remember that." And he left the room to go and fetch Darius.

12 A New Kind Of Harvest

Daylight had also arrived on Terra. The next thing Shannon knew, she was being woken up by her mother, who was asking her why she wasn't dressed for school yet.

"Come on, Shannon, it's really late," repeated her mother from the doorway of Shannon's bedroom. "What's the matter with you this morning? You never normally miss breakfast." Shannon looked up at her groggily, struggling to wake up.

"I don't know…" she started to reply, and then in a rush she remembered everything that had happened the night before.

I can't go to school, she thought. I just can't. She felt quite panicky at the thought of having to pretend that everything was normal and face Penny's questions. I can't just go on with an ordinary day. Not when Jax and Darius are facing who knows what back on Androva, she thought.

"I don't feel very well..." she began. Her mother took a step into the room to take a closer look at her daughter. Fortunately for Shannon, she looked completely exhausted, with shadows under her eyes and very pale skin. All of this made her story about feeling unwell appear quite believable. Her mother was soon convinced and agreed to call the school to explain that Shannon would not be in that day.

I must look really bad, thought Shannon guiltily. She had never told a serious lie to her parents before, but then she reasoned that this was not really lying. She just wasn't going to mention anything about Androva and her adventures of the day and night before.

If she did decide to tell the whole truth about what had happened to her, then her parents probably would think she *was* lying. Much better to just say she was feeling ill, and leave it at that.

Eventually the house was quiet, Shannon's father having left for work, and Shannon's mother to take Tammy to school. By this time Shannon had fallen asleep again, unable to fight the weariness of her late night and travel back through the portal. She dozed off and on for most of the morning, and finally woke up properly at lunchtime.

When she realised how late it was, she was really annoyed with herself for having slept for so long. Her mother had brought her a sandwich and a drink, and she had this for her lunch, before taking a quick shower and getting dressed. Finally ready, she sat down to think.

Before falling asleep the previous night, she had come up with half of an idea about what to do next. She knew that the stronger her magic was, the better the chance she had of helping Jax and Darius if she ever got the chance to return to Androva. So surely the most constructive thing she could do was to build up her magic somehow. If she could just figure out how to do that...

Then it came to her. Maybe she could harvest some magic of her own!

She sat up straighter, feeling excited. It made perfect sense. Here she was, wanting additional magic, and she lived in a world which apparently had plenty of living magic in its trees. And she just happened to be right next to an area of woodland. Even better, she was an underage magician, which meant she should have the ability to harvest magic.

She considered this, twirling a strand of hair around her fingers. When she had seen Jax and Darius the first time, Jax had created a glowing silver ball out of the magic they were harvesting. It had seemed as if they would carry it back just like that.

She recalled what Darius had said about the Repository of Magic. If this was where the harvest receipts were counted, then the magic obviously had to be taken there.

She wanted to do something different. She didn't want to create something out of the harvested magic that she could hold and carry. She wanted to capture it and combine it with her own magic somehow. She had no idea if this was even possible, but she was determined to give it a try.

"Mum?" she called, walking out of her room and down the stairs.

"What is it?" responded her mother from the dining room, where she was working that afternoon. Shannon's mother ran her own business making personalised greeting cards, and Shannon could see that she was in the middle of a complicated order.

"I thought I might get some fresh air," said Shannon, "take a quick walk in the woods or something."

"You are looking much better," observed her mother. "If you're well enough to go out for a walk, then you can definitely go back to school tomorrow. Maybe you could ask Penny to come over when school finishes so that you can catch up on today's assignments?"

"Mu-um!" protested Shannon.

Her mother gave an amused smile. "That's the deal. No walk unless you agree to catch up on your schoolwork."

Shannon reluctantly agreed. Perhaps Penny won't be able to make it anyway, she thought. She decided to worry about it later, and after putting on her trainers, she made her way out of the house and towards the woods.

There was a particular clearing that she was headed for. It had a large fallen tree in the middle of it, wide and smooth enough to walk along. She and her sister had often used it to pretend to be gymnasts walking along their very own balance beam. There were many large trees surrounding this clearing, and Shannon thought it would be a good place to start her experiment.

When she arrived, she turned around in a slow circle, looking up at the trees until she felt a bit dizzy. They were tall and green in the spring sunshine, and their leaves made a whispering noise, almost as if the trees were telling secrets to each other.

"OK," she said under her breath. "Time to find out if this is going to work..."

She started by projecting her magic outwards until her hands were glowing. With a sense of relief, she noticed that this was becoming easier and easier to do. The complicated Deceiving Spell that had taken so much of her concentration the previous night did not seem to have diminished her ability. If anything, her magic felt stronger.

She walked over to the tallest tree and moved one hand slowly towards it until she could feel a low buzzing. It gave off a faint glow that gradually became brighter and brighter. Shannon felt her fingertips tingling, almost as if they had pins and needles.

After a short while, when the tree's glow was as strong as she thought it was going to get, Shannon began to step backwards, drawing the bright light with her. Soon she was shimmering from head to toe, and she closed her eyes to concentrate.

She focused on the magic spark deep inside her mind, and used it like a magnet, in the same way that Jax had taught her for the Scattering Spell defence.

Gradually all the light surrounding her was drawn in by the magic spark, until there was none left. Cautiously Shannon opened her eyes and looked down at herself. Had it worked? She tried to project her magic outwards again, and the speed with which her hands lit up this time made her gasp.

They were almost fluorescent. She grinned triumphantly and clenched her fists. "*Yes!*" she whispered.

Shannon repeated the process twice more with different trees, to be absolutely certain that she had harvested as much magic as possible in the time she had. Then she reluctantly decided that she would have to go back to text Penny before school ended.

She was halfway up the path to her house when she stopped suddenly. Before continuing, she took a moment to suppress her force field. She had to make sure that there was no chance anything would start glowing once she was back in the house.

Penny was only too delighted to hear from Shannon, and quickly agreed to come round after school with that day's homework. Shannon had decided that she might as well meet with Penny. Now that she had successfully carried out her plan, she felt more able to behave normally for the rest of the day.

It was unlikely that anything would happen with Androva until nightfall, she reasoned. It would be a brave Androvan magician who made a daylight trip to Terra now.

Penny arrived and began to excitedly relate the events of the day to Shannon. Apparently one of the older children had set off the fire alarm as a joke that morning, and lessons had been completely disrupted all the way up to lunch time. Shannon listened to her friend, realising how much she had changed in the last two days. She would once have found this story as entertaining as Penny did, but now she was only mildly interested.

Everything seemed very unimportant compared to the nightmare that Jax and Darius were facing back on Androva. The homework was fortunately not too difficult, and Shannon and Penny had soon completed it. Shannon's mother suggested they take a drink into the garden while she went to collect Tammy from her after-school club.

"OK then, tell me what's really going on," began Penny, once they were alone. "Something's been up with you for over a week now, and I want to know what it is." She gave Shannon a challenging look.

Shannon looked back without replying. She agreed that Penny was entitled to an explanation. They knew each other so well, and it was not fair to Penny that Shannon had been so distant recently. But Shannon could not tell her about any of it. There was no way that Penny could possibly understand. Shannon was just about to make up a story about some kind of family problem, when a voice came from the garden.

"Stand up, girl, and come with me," it demanded. Shannon turned in the direction of the voice and jumped out of her chair, spilling her drink as she did so. It landed on the paving slabs with a crash, and the glass shattered into several pieces.

She realised immediately that it was a magician from Androva. His black shirt was engraved with an elaborate Sygnus in the shape of a sun. The centre was spinning. He had an unfriendly look on his face.

Shannon quickly looked at Penny to see her reaction to this sudden arrival.

"Don't be a fool," said the man dismissively. "She cannot see me. I repeat, *come with me*," he continued, not raising his voice, but somehow managing to sound even more unpleasant. For a second, Shannon contemplated trying to run, but the next second she felt the icy steel band of an extremely powerful Containment Spell inside her head. Immediately the pressure increased, and she almost fell to her knees with the sudden pain.

"What's the matter, are you OK?" Penny asked, and at this the man raised one glowing hand towards her and said "Go."

Penny paused, and said in a rush, "I completely forgot, I have to be home to help my mum with something!"

Running into the house to pick up her school bag, she called back, "Sorry, I have to go!" and Shannon heard the front door close behind her. Looking at her captor, she realised that he had just performed a very effective Distraction Dpell on Penny.

"Now," he said impatiently, "you will come with me." Hearing the magician speak again, Shannon was now sure about something. It was Marcus.

13 Punishment

Shannon tried to overcome her fear as she followed Marcus towards the portal. At first she was so scared that she kept forgetting not to fight the Containment Spell, and the resulting pain made her walk very unsteadily. Marcus turned back to wait for her, annoyed.

"Reports of your abilities have clearly been exaggerated," he said, and then he gave a spiteful laugh. "I feel almost sorry for you, Terran. You are involved in something that you cannot possibly understand."

He waited for her to catch up with him, and gave her a push, and she stumbled into the portal, landing on her knees on the spellstation that was waiting on the other side. Scrambling to her feet as the shimmer receded, she realised she was in a very different portal room to the one she had visited with Jax.

This was much larger and brighter, with a

greater number of symbols. There were silver embellishments where the ceiling met the walls, and again where the walls met the floor. Three magicians stood against the far wall, apparently waiting for her arrival.

"You may relax, friends," said Marcus. "This girl is no threat to any of us."

At hearing these words, Shannon felt her anger start to grow, until it began to outweigh her fear. Don't underestimate me, she thought. She remembered again how Marcus had treated Jax the night before, and her anger intensified.

Gradually she was able to suppress the magic in her head until the band stopped hurting so much. She didn't go too far though, as she wanted Marcus to believe that his Containment Spell was still very much operational. At least he didn't seem to have noticed the extra magic that she had harvested.

Shannon decided to do exactly as she was told, to make sure Marcus continued to believe that she was weak and unable to defend herself. And besides, she wanted to find out where Jax and Darius were being held before she did anything. There were so many questions she would have liked to ask, but knowing that Marcus was very unlikely to tell her anything, she kept silent.

He hurried her out of the portal room and down a large well-lit corridor. Then, as she had half expected, they climbed up a steep circular staircase. It seemed that all portal rooms were located underground, no matter how grand they were.

Little by little, Shannon felt the usual tiredness sweep over her. She had made five trips through the portal in two days, and this trip was proving to be just as exhausting as the rest.

Frantically she tried to think of something she could do to stop the tiredness, but she was already using up a lot of energy concentrating on the Containment Spell. She had to resist the band Marcus had created just enough to make him think that she was still under his control. The tiredness kept on increasing, and so she made a decision. She deliberately stumbled and fell over.

"What are you doing, girl?" snapped Marcus, looking over his shoulder as he heard her fall. The other three magicians, who had been following them, stopped and looked down at her suspiciously.

Shannon closed her eyes. "So tired," she mumbled, and pretended to fall asleep. Marcus tried tightening the band of his Containment Spell to wake her up, but somehow she managed to keep her eyes closed and her face still.

"She is unconscious," confirmed Marcus. "It must be the portal. Her resistance really is incredibly low. If I didn't know better, I would start to doubt the boy's interrogation data…"

Shannon pricked up her ears at this. Interrogation data? About her? And was it from Jax or Darius?

"Well, don't just stand there," said Marcus crossly. "One of you go and get a Portal Remedy. She's no use to us at the Assembly like this!"

Shannon was relieved to hear that her plan was working. She had pretended to fall asleep because she thought it was the quickest way to get hold of a Portal Remedy. She had not wanted to gradually get more and more tired. What if the opportunity to escape came along and she was too exhausted to take it? She wanted to feel back to normal as soon as possible.

In a few minutes she felt something forcing her mouth open and the familiar sweetness of the Portal Remedy being poured inside. Still pretending, she coughed and spluttered a bit as if it were waking her up. Soon she felt her strength coming back.

"OK, get up," demanded Marcus, hauling her to her feet. "I refuse to be late just because some stupid Terran girl who is pretending to be a magician can't stay awake long enough to make it down the hallway."

Shannon kept her eyes lowered in case Marcus saw the laughter in them. No more than you deserve, she thought. She continued to walk very slowly, just to see if she could annoy him a bit more. They passed several doorways leading off the corridor, but continued right to the end. Here was the largest doorway, engraved with the words "Council Examination Rooms."

Marcus pushed it open to reveal a small hexagonal chamber with six doors evenly spaced in its walls, including the door they had just walked through. She just had the chance to notice that the doors on her left were engraved as Interrogation Rooms 1-3, but did not have time to look to the right. Marcus continued to a door called "Assembly" and opened it.

They entered a large high-ceilinged room with tall windows and pillars in each corner. The walls and floor were made from white polished stone. There was a long desk made from the same stone on the far side of the room, shaped in a gently curving arc. This allowed the magicians seated behind it to see each other as well as the room in front of them.

There were twenty high-backed chairs of equal size behind the desk, each made out of a very dark, intricately carved wood. Four chairs were empty, and the three magicians who had followed Marcus and Shannon from the portal room hurried across to fill them. Shannon guessed that the final empty chair belonged to Marcus. This must be the Council.

"Thank you for your patience, friends," said Marcus, walking forwards. He turned to point to Shannon. "As you can see, I have brought the girl. I am delighted to report that she is no threat whatsoever to Androva. It is clear, however, that she has knowledge of us, and of magic. Knowledge that she could not have obtained without a violation of the Code. We can now prove, once and for all, the offences of the underage magician known as Jax."

At this, Shannon noticed one of the Council members briefly bow his head. She guessed that he was Revus, Jax's father.

"Now," continued Marcus, his voice taking on a rather complacent tone, "you have already heard the interrogation data of the boy, Darius, who verified that Jax did travel to Terra, alone, and returned with this Terran girl you see before you.

"Darius believes that she is a magician of some ability. I can assure you that she is not." At this he turned to look at Shannon scornfully. Shannon gritted her teeth.

Wait, she told herself. You can't take on the entire Council.

Marcus continued. "According to Darius, they then proceeded to use an Unauthorised Spell to enter the restricted section of the Repository of Records and read the treaty. Each of these offences on its own is enough to justify a severe punishment. Together, they are unforgivable."

He paused to make sure the Council members understood, while Shannon tried to hide her shock. Darius had told Marcus everything! How could he do that, after all he had said about friendship and being part of a team?

"I travelled to Terra myself to retrieve this girl. Whatever her limited magical ability, she obviously knows enough about Androva to corroborate Darius's interrogation. I suggest we now bring the boys forward."

Shannon's heart leapt at this. She really wanted to see Jax and Darius to find out if they were alright. Particularly Jax. She had noticed that Marcus did not refer to Jax's interrogation. Maybe Jax had refused to tell Marcus anything?

Marcus walked back to the doorway, presumably to fetch the two boys. One of the Council members half rose from her chair and called out, "Marcus! Are you sure the girl is secure?"

Marcus turned and lifted his hand, which immediately glowed brighter. Shannon realised what he was going to do a second before he did it.

He was going to tighten the Containment Spell to demonstrate that she was no threat. She braced herself for the pain, having decided to allow him to go ahead.

If she were going to have any chance of escaping later, it was important that everyone believed in her lack of ability. He was ruthless. Despite the fact that Shannon was prepared for it, she cried out, and this time she did actually fall to her knees when the band tightened.

"Stop this, Marcus," came the voice of another magician. "Your word is enough. You do not have to provide a demonstration as well."

Shannon straightened back up again with relief as the pressure in her head decreased. She was developing a terrible headache though. She guessed that without the blue haze of a Protection Spell, as they'd had in the training room at Jax's house, Marcus could really hurt her.

Marcus, not looking at all sorry for what he had just done, left the room. There was a short silence, and Shannon glanced at the faces of the Council members in front of her.

There was a mix of men and women of various ages, though most were older. All had quite serious expressions, and a few looked disapproving. She turned at the sound of the door opening again, and Marcus reappeared.

Behind him walked Darius, and alongside him Jax. Darius looked tired and unhappy, but it was Jax's appearance that upset Shannon the most.

He was incredibly pale and looked utterly

exhausted. As he got closer, he noticed Shannon, and at first he looked shocked. Then his shock turned to anger, and he glared at Darius, who miserably lowered his gaze.

Then Shannon knew for sure what had happened. Jax had somehow resisted his interrogation. So he knew that the only way Shannon could have been brought back to Androva so quickly was if Darius had told Marcus all about her.

Jax might not even have known that Darius had taken her back in the first place, Shannon realised. He might be thinking that Darius and Shannon hadn't escaped the Repository of Records at all. Either way, he was obviously very disappointed in his friend.

Marcus was looking at them with a smile. "I suppose you are wondering how I found your little Terran friend so quickly," he said to Jax. "It was all thanks to Darius here. All the details you refused to tell me, I learned from him. We know everything."

He turned to face the Council. "And so, my friends, I hereby recommend that the Spell of Removal is performed immediately."

There was a shocked murmur among the Council, at the same time as Shannon and Darius cried, "No!"

Darius continued, pointing at Marcus. "You

can't do this. You told me that if I confessed everything, you would spare him the Spell of Removal so that he could continue magic-taking. You *promised* me!" His voice was trembling, and he looked on the verge of tears.

Marcus raised his eyebrows as if he were mildly surprised. "I can assure you I never made any such promise," he said calmly.

"You're lying!" shouted Darius.

Marcus leaned forwards and said menacingly, "If you don't wish to suffer the same punishment, I suggest you *close your mouth*."

Darius started to speak again, but as Jax shook his head, he stopped. "There's no point," whispered Jax.

Shannon looked at Marcus, feeling her anger building again. She knew Darius was telling the truth.

The Council held a short debate. Some members were worried about the quota, and argued that all underage magicians were required for harvesting just now, whatever their offences. Revus in particular emphasised this line of reasoning.

There were others who argued that punishing Jax might somehow repair the breaking of the treaty and return the harvests to normal. Finally the Council voted. There were nine votes against the punishment and eleven votes in favour of it.

Marcus, looking delighted with himself, prepared to project the spell.

14 After The Spell

Jax looked across at Shannon. "I'm sorry," he mouthed, with a weaker version of his old smile. Then he lifted his head and faced Marcus, determined that he would not give Marcus the satisfaction of seeing his fear.

"Stand aside," Marcus instructed Darius, and Darius slowly stepped away from Jax. Then Marcus raised both hands, and Shannon knew it was now or never.

She quickly escaped the Containment Spell inside her head. Then, just as Marcus began to project the glow of the Spell of Removal towards Jax, she said, "Stop."

She spoke very softly, and half of the Council members did not hear her. But they certainly saw what happened next. Shannon used every single bit of magic she had inside her to send the Spell of Immobility racing towards Marcus.

And it worked. The glow that had started to

ALEX C VICK

project from Marcus was totally frozen, hanging in the air as if it really had been turned to ice. At first no one knew what had happened. Marcus's expression was almost comical as he tried again to push his spell outwards. Jax looked at him for a moment, then half laughed in disbelief.

Turning to see who had projected the spell, he realised in amazement that it was Shannon. Shannon was starting to enjoy herself. She became aware that she didn't need to use all of her magic to hold the spell in place after all, so she toned it down a bit.

She grinned at Jax, and her usually solemn brown eyes were sparkling with glee. Jax was laughing properly by now, and the Council members whispered to each other in consternation.

Revus was the first to get up out of his seat and cross the room to take a closer look, and he instantly understood that Marcus was being held by a very powerful Spell of Immobility. What Revus couldn't quite believe was that the spell was coming from the Terran girl. And not only that, but she was showing no signs of struggling. She looked as if she could hold the spell all day.

"Marcus, old friend," began Revus, resting his hand on Marcus's shoulder. Marcus produced a sort of gurgling noise of frustrated rage deep in his throat, the only sound that he was able to make. Revus continued. "It seems *possible* the girl is somewhat more powerful than you thought."

On hearing this, Darius tried not to laugh as well. Revus went on. "The Council was clearly not in possession of all the facts when we made our vote on this punishment." Turning to the other Council members, he said, "I propose we postpone until we have had the chance to examine these new developments." Every single Council member agreed.

Revus lifted his hand from Marcus's shoulder and gave it a pat. "I'll assume that you would be in agreement with us in light of this new information," he said kindly. Then he walked across to Shannon and said to her, "I think you can stop now, you've made your point." Leaning closer so that only she could hear him, he breathed, "*Thank you.*"

Shannon reluctantly released Marcus. As soon as he was completely free of the spell, he roared, "HOW DARE YOU?" and started to lift his hands as if to project a spell back to her in retaliation. Then he seemed to remember where he was, and looked back at the rest of the Council.

Awkwardly, he lowered his hands again and, still flushed red with anger, had to make do with muttering a few threats under his breath.

Jax, overcome with relief that he was still a

magician, at least for now, gave Marcus a scornful look. Then he walked over to Shannon and smiled at her in amazement. Pushing a strand of her hair away from her face, he said quietly, "Who's the greatest underage magician the world has ever seen now?"

Shannon smiled back, so thankful that he was OK that she didn't know what to say. They hugged quickly, a bit embarrassed. Revus watched them thoughtfully, realising there was a bond between them that was stronger than he had imagined when he had first heard Darius's interrogation data earlier that day. Further investigation into this whole situation was obviously necessary.

Darius approached Jax, nervous of the reception he would get now that Jax knew he had told Marcus all about Shannon. Jax tried not to be angry with Darius. He understood that Darius had thought he was doing the right thing. And besides, Jax could hardly complain at the way it had all turned out. So he half smiled at Darius, and Darius returned the smile with relief.

The Assembly broke up until the following day to allow Revus time to interrogate the three underage magicians. All the Council were happy to allow Revus to take charge. Except for Marcus of course, but he was too sensible to voice his opinion.

Revus had long been a respected member of the Council. Though he was Jax's father, he had proved again that his duties to the Council came first, when he had allowed Marcus to go ahead with the Spell of Removal a few moments before. Therefore the Council was convinced that Revus could be entrusted with the interrogation.

The Mortification of Marcus, as it became known, was eventually retold to all future generations of underage magicians. It served as a warning to always double-check your facts, and to never be over confident. Poor Marcus had always wanted to be recognised for his work on the Council. And this story did make him famous, though perhaps not quite in the way he would have wished.

But before any questioning could start, Jax and Darius needed to rest. Revus could see that his son was starting to sway on his feet with exhaustion, and Darius was not coping much better. So he made the decision to take them to Darius's house.

This was not too far from the Council offices, and it would mean that the two boys could sleep for a few hours. Darius's parents were waiting outside the Council examination rooms. They were anxious for some news of their son after his removal from the house by Marcus the night before. Revus thought that he would explain everything to Marek and Iona while the boys slept.

Council Assemblies were usually conducted in secrecy, but Revus saw no need to keep Darius's parents in the dark. Iona had already proved herself trustworthy by not telling anyone about her former prophecy work with the Council. And Marek knew the seriousness of the incomplete harvest quota, because of his job in the Repository of Magic. Further secrecy seemed a bit pointless in this case.

As for the girl... Revus still hadn't decided what to do about her. She did not seem to have suffered the same lack of sleep as the two boys, but they had a long night ahead of them with the interrogation. He decided that she should probably try to get some rest as well.

Revus waited until the last remaining Council members had left the Assembly Room, then turned to Shannon, Jax, and Darius to explain what would happen next. Jax and Darius did not protest. Now that the drama of the Assembly had passed, they were both struggling to stay awake. Darius was also glad of the chance to see his parents.

Shannon, whose confidence levels were not so high now that her anger towards Marcus had died down, nervously opened her mouth to speak.

"What about my parents? Marcus just brought

me here with no warning. They'll probably be thinking the worst by now," she finished unhappily.

"What have your parents got to do with any of this?" Revus started impatiently, and then, seeing the girl's forlorn face, he reconsidered. He was not accustomed to giving any thought to the lives and concerns of the inhabitants of Terra. But after what this girl had just done to save his son, he was in her debt. He beckoned one of the custodians who had entered to clear up the room. "Go and get Aaron," he instructed.

In a short while, a young man with brown hair and a pleasant expression appeared. He looked at Revus expectantly. "I want you to travel to Terra as soon as nightfall is completely upon us," said Revus. "You will go to the location most recently visited by Marcus. You can find this in the portal records of the Council spellstation underneath this building.

"There will be a house nearby, where you will find a Terran family. Please use your strongest Distraction Spell to ensure that they experience no concern about the disappearance of their daughter."

Aaron nodded willingly. He was known for his ability to project excellent Distraction Spells, and as a Council custodian he was also accustomed to unusual requests. He promised to do as Revus had asked, and left the room. Shannon sighed with relief. "Thank you," she said earnestly. Then she looked uncertain. "Is it OK to send a magician to use a spell on my parents? That's not breaking the Code, is it?"

"Aaron will not be detected," said Revus. "And don't you think it's a bit late to worry about the Code now?" he continued, raising one eyebrow.

"That's not fair," countered Shannon hotly. "I didn't know anything about the Code..." She trailed off, hanging her head. It was true that she hadn't known about the Code when she'd first got involved with Jax. But she realised she *had* known all about it when she broke into the restricted section of the Repository of Records. And it hadn't stopped her.

Jax, still standing next to Shannon, gave her a sympathetic look. "Don't worry," he whispered to her. "My father is very good at making you feel stupid. He used to do it to me all the time."

"I suggest we leave," said Revus. "Now is not the time to debate this. I will conduct the interrogation later." He led the way out of the Assembly Room and towards the entrance of the Council offices. Iona and Marek exclaimed at the sight of their son, relieved to see him, but worried about his weary appearance.

When Shannon had realised that these were

Darius's parents, she had expected them to ask some questions about her—who she was for starters! Neither said anything, but they obviously knew more than they were letting on. Marek looked at her in complete shock, almost as if he had seen a ghost. Iona just nodded to herself and seemed satisfied about something. Shannon found it all very strange.

During the short walk, Shannon tried to take in as much as she could about Landor. It was not quite evening, so there was enough daylight to see a lot more of her surroundings than she had been able to in the darkness of the night before. The buildings were all rather different in shape and colour, though most had the same steep slate roofs.

The streets were clean, but quite uneven, and there were no cars or any other vehicles to be seen anywhere. Shannon supposed that magicians had no need for cars to get around. There must be many spells that they could use to travel from one location to another.

Their group attracted a few curious glances, but for the most part no one paid them much attention. Everyone Shannon saw seemed very polite and quiet, but perhaps that was because Revus was a well-known Council member? It all made her feel a bit unsettled because it was so different to the hustle and bustle that she was used to at home.

What Shannon didn't realise was that by this time most people were starting to feel afraid. Androvans had always known about the Evil that lingered in the background of their lives. It was like a sense of foreboding that nobody could quite ignore.

Despite this, life on Androva was usually lively and happy. But now that rumours about the harvest quota were starting to circulate, that sense of foreboding was turning into real fear.

Within five minutes of arriving at the house, the boys were asleep. Shannon, in a room next door, lay awake for a little while. She heard the rumble of voices downstairs as Revus explained the events of the Assembly to Iona and Marek. Even though she had been sure that she would not easily sleep again, it was not long before the voices jumbled together with the mixed-up thoughts in her head, and she drifted off.

The next thing she knew, she was being woken up by a hand on her arm. She was completely disorientated for a few seconds, and, panicking, she opened her mouth to scream.

"Hey, it's OK," said Jax softly. "It's just me, it's OK." His green eyes gleamed in the light coming through the doorway.

Shannon took a deep breath to calm herself down. "How long have I been asleep for?" she asked, sitting up and trying to rearrange her hair into some sort of order.

"I don't know," replied Jax, "I've only just woken up myself."

"Where's Darius?"

"Still sleeping," answered Jax. "I'm sorry I woke you up, but I need to talk to you before all the craziness starts up again."

15 Before The Interrogation

Jax sat on the edge of the bed. "Firstly, how amazing were *you* in the Assembly earlier? I've never seen anything so fantastic in my life. I'll remember the look on Marcus's face until I die!"

Shannon smiled. "It felt pretty good to me as well," she admitted. "Once I realised I could hold the spell quite easily, I actually loved it. After the way he had treated us all… it was exactly what he deserved."

"Do you know what he said to me?" Jax asked. "He said 'I always win.' I wish I could talk to him now and tell him that he doesn't. 'I *nearly* always win' doesn't sound quite so impressive, does it?"

Shannon laughed. "I'm just relieved you're OK," she said fervently. "I was going crazy wondering what was happening to you."

Jax smiled back at her. "I'm relieved I taught you the Spell of Immobility," he said in return. "I almost decided we didn't have time.

"By the way, I figured out how you were able to activate my Sygnus key," he continued. "It's been bugging me for ages. It was obvious once I thought about it. There are supposed to be preventive spells in place to stop underage activation. And they work. I've never been able to do it before. Not that I've tried," he said hastily.

Then with a grin, he added, "At least I haven't tried that often. The preventive spell must be located in the Sygnus itself. As long as I am wearing my Sygnus, it works to prevent me from activating it.

"Kind of clever really. I can't activate it unless I'm wearing it, but when I'm wearing it, the spell stops me. You don't have one—a Sygnus I mean—so the preventive spell doesn't work on you. And once mine was unlocked the first time, the spell was weaker."

Shannon considered this, and agreed with Jax. It did make sense. Then she turned away.

"What is it?" asked Jax.

Shannon hesitated for a moment. "This might sound stupid, but I really wish I'd brought my toothbrush with me," she muttered, a bit embarrassed.

"Your toothbrush?" repeated Jax, mystified. "What is a toothbrush?"

"You know, to clean your teeth!" said

Shannon, her embarrassment making her raise her voice.

"Oh, I see," replied Jax, struggling not to smile. "Well, why don't you just use a Cleaning Spell instead? They work on everything. Clothes, hair, faces... even teeth."

He raised one softly glowing hand, and a silvery light began to spin in the air, round and round, until it reached Shannon. Then it expanded, encasing her from head to toe for a few seconds, still spinning. She made a small yelp of surprise, and then almost before she knew it, the spell had finished. It was quite remarkable.

Everything felt clean and brand new. Even her hair was smooth, something which very rarely happened without straighteners. She touched it self-consciously.

"You look great," said Jax shyly, and Shannon's cheeks went a bit pink.

"I've been trying to figure out a few things too, and I have a question for you," she said, twirling her hair again.

"Ask me anything," replied Jax, his old mischievous grin firmly back in place. They sat side by side on the bed, their shoulders touching.

"All that stuff you and Darius were telling me yesterday about the difficulties you had harvesting the same amount of magic as before. Can you explain to me exactly how it works when you harvest magic?"

Shannon had been wondering about this ever since her attack on Marcus had been such a runaway success. If the magic-takers had been struggling as much as Jax had told her they were, then how was it possible that she had become so much more powerful?

Surely the amount that she had been able to take from the trees would also have been reduced? The best she had hoped for was that she would become a bit stronger, but it now seemed that she had done a lot more than that.

"Well, when we harvest magic, we kind of draw it out from the trees using our spark," started Jax.

Shannon waited for him to continue, as she had already guessed this part.

"Then we use a Controlling Spell, which draws it all together. I always turn it into a ball shape, but some magicians create a cube or a cylinder— it depends on how your Controlling Spell works. The main thing is that you have to be able to carry it easily in your hand without squashing it or anything."

"Why?" asked Shannon curiously. "What happens if you squash it?"

"It's very fragile," answered Jax. "Any pressure can damage it really easily. Basically, once you've collected the harvest, you have to get it to the

Repository of Magic as fast as possible. The longer you wait, the smaller it gets. So the worst thing you can do is wait around, or drop it, or hold it too tightly."

Shannon pondered this. "What was the problem with the harvest last night then? Did you collect less in the first place, or did it just get small really quickly?"

"That's actually a great question," said Jax thoughtfully. "You're the first person to ask me that." He frowned, trying to remember. "I would say that the problem was that it deteriorated faster. It's hard to be totally sure because it happened so fast. But I'm pretty certain that the magic I collected was the same as ever in the very first moment. By the time I reached the Repository it was much smaller than usual, even though I was really careful."

So that's why, thought Shannon. That's why the magic I collected was still so powerful. I didn't try to control it or carry it, I just merged with it and it became part of me.

"What is it?" asked Jax, looking at Shannon's face, which was lit up with excitement. Shannon opened her mouth, about to tell him all about it, when they were interrupted by Darius. He pushed the door wide open, rubbing his eyes.

"What's going on?" he said sleepily. "Did I miss anything?"

"What do you mean, since your spectacular interrogation failure?" asked Jax, his earlier anger returning as he remembered what Marcus had done to him during the long hours of questioning. "Just for the record," Jax continued, "the next time I resist an entire night of interrogation, please don't turn up at the last minute and give away all our secrets! You know that Marcus can't be trusted to be fair where I'm concerned."

Darius hung his head for a moment, but Shannon scowled at Jax, saying "If Darius hadn't confessed, I wouldn't be here, and you might not still be a magician! So let's forget about it, shall we?"

Jax reluctantly apologised, as did Darius (much less reluctantly). "I can't imagine what your interrogation must have been like," offered Shannon softly, trying to mollify Jax. "At first you saved us in the Repository of Records when you gave yourself up. And then you saved us again when you refused to talk to Marcus. We understand how big a deal that was. It's just that reliving it won't help us now."

Jax looked at her, grateful for her understanding. His anger went away. He repeated his apology to Darius, with more sincerity this time.

Then Jax remembered that Shannon had been

about to tell him something. He was about to ask her what it was, when Darius cut in.

"I need to tell you what I heard my parents talking about last night," he began urgently, looking over his shoulder to check that they were still alone. "After I went back through the portal, I returned home to try to find out more about what was going on."

"Wait a minute!" said Shannon. "I thought you were captured when you stepped back into the portal? I saw someone grab you!"

"Yes, that's true," said Darius. So much had happened since then that he had almost forgotten that Revus had been there waiting for him. "But it was only Jax's father. He was looking for Jax. Dorian must have just delivered the message from Marcus."

"And he let you go?" said Jax suspiciously.

"Yes, he did," confirmed Darius. "I think he was too worried about you to notice that I was alone."

"I can't believe that," scoffed Jax.

"Well, you should," said Shannon firmly. "Just because he follows the rules, it doesn't mean that he doesn't care about you. He thanked me for what I did to Marcus."

Jax was genuinely amazed to hear this, and he stopped to reconsider. Then he shrugged as if he were unconcerned, but inwardly he was smiling.

"Anyway, I saw my mother reading a prophecy when I got home," said Darius.

"What?" asked Shannon. Looking at Jax, she saw that he was not surprised by Darius's words. "Reading a *prophecy*?"

Darius, with another worried glance over his shoulder, quickly explained to her how prophecy reading worked on Androva. Shannon shook her head incredulously. Just when she thought she was starting to understand this crazy world, something new came up that was even stranger.

"What was the prophecy about?" prompted Jax.

"Us," said Darius. "It was about us." He tried to remember exactly what his mother had said. "My mother said that the future of Androva was still uncertain, but that without 'this girl,' the future would be sure to take a darker turn. She also said that you and I were involved, Jax, but she couldn't see exactly how. The girl she mentioned was you, Shannon. I saw a figure that looked exactly like you in the Prophecy story."

Before either Jax or Shannon had the chance to respond to what Darius had said, they heard footsteps on the stairs. It was Marek.

"Good," he said, "you're all awake." He drew his son out of the room and spoke to him in a low voice. "Darius, I have to leave now for the Repository. The night's harvests are starting to come in, and I have to be there to make the count. I wanted to tell you before I left that whatever happens, your mother and I will support you as best we can. There is so much about what is happening that we don't yet understand, but we will find a way through this together."

He gave Darius a brief hug, and turned away.

Darius watched his father leave with mixed emotions. This was the first time his father had spoken to him this way, almost like an equal, which was kind of amazing. Whatever Marek had heard from Revus, it had obviously made him look at his son in a different way. But Darius was also sad that there was no time to appreciate this change. He hoped that he would see his father again before the night was over.

"What did he say to you?" asked Jax interestedly.

Darius shook his head. "Ask me again later," he murmured.

Revus called for them to come downstairs. Iona was waiting with some hot food and drink, and all three ate and drank gratefully. Jax and Darius looked almost back to normal after the meal, though the shadows under Jax's eyes remained. Revus patiently waited for them to finish eating. Shannon couldn't tell what he was thinking, as his expression remained calm and unreadable.

She was longing to ask Jax and Darius what they thought about the prophecy. But because neither of them was saying anything, she decided to remain silent too.

"Now," said Revus, "before we proceed with the interrogation, I have decided that you need to hear a certain story. Normally you would not hear this until you come of age. But in light of some information that Iona has given me, regarding a prophecy that she has seen over and over again in recent days, I am persuaded to let you hear this story tonight."

16 The Evil (Part One)

Iona began to speak. "Once upon a time…" she started, then she paused and smiled at Shannon. "Isn't that how all the most famous stories start?" she asked. Shannon nodded.

Jax and Darius looked puzzled. "There was a time," continued Iona, "when storybooks were permitted here on Androva, but not since the treaty. It was thought that encouraging the imaginations of our underage magicians was a bad idea, and might lead to more problems in the future.

"There are still a handful to be found in the restricted section of the Repository of Records, but that is all. You can make up your own minds about that when you've heard *this* story."

"But my world—I mean Terra—we got to keep our storybooks, didn't we?" said Shannon, already knowing the answer, but wanting to understand a bit more about it.

"Yes," confirmed Iona. "I always thought it was a sad thing. Terra would keep all its stories, and fairy tales, and fictions, and could write hundreds more. As many as it wished. But without magic, they would always remain stories. No one would ever be able to bring them to life."

Jax thought back to the night when he had seen Shannon transfixed by her book. It had aroused his curiosity so much that the next time he had returned in daylight to find out more.

If Androva had not forbidden storybooks, he might not have been so curious about the one that Shannon was reading. And it was the hero in the book that Shannon had lent him who had inspired him again. Perhaps the Terran books were not as powerless as Iona imagined.

"But that's not true!" Shannon was arguing. "You can still bring them to life, even if it's only in your imagination. I have read stories that made me feel like I was actually there, living the story alongside the characters."

She blushed a little. I sound like such a bookworm, she thought. Well, so what if I am? I'm not ashamed of it, either.

"What I mean to say is please don't pity me, or anyone else who likes a good story. Magic isn't the only thing that makes life interesting, you know…"

Iona looked apologetic. "I am sorry, Shannon.

We have a tendency on Androva to think that Terra came off worst after the treaty."

"I get why you would think that," Shannon said. "When I first learned that I was a magician, I thought it was all amazing and wonderful and that my life before was boring. But the more I learn about Androva, the more I can see that it's not all great here.

"You've been living with the responsibility of containing this Evil, whatever it is, for hundreds of years. And Terra didn't have to worry about that. OK, we're not magicians, but some of the things we can do now would have seemed like magic to the Terrans who signed the treaty. I mean, we're not exactly stuck in the Dark Ages, are we?" she challenged.

"No, you are not," Iona agreed with a smile. The more she saw of Shannon, the more the prophecy made sense to her. Iona would have to rethink most of her beliefs about Terra and its inhabitants, if this girl was anything to go by. She paused for a moment, then recommenced the story.

"Once upon a time there were magicians on both Androva and Terra. Magic was an essential part of everyday life on both worlds. Spells were used for everything from travel, to growing crops and influencing the weather, to building houses, creating good luck and bad luck, and even physical transformation. There was a natural hierarchy of magic skills, with some able to become master magicians, and some having only the most basic abilities. There were even some people that shunned the use of magic altogether."

What Iona was describing was all unsurprising to Jax and Darius, except for the small fact that she included Terra in the story. They remembered what they had read in the treaty. It seemed that there really had been a time when magicians lived on Terra. For Shannon, hearing the use of magic on her world spoken about in such matter-of-fact terms was a bit disconcerting.

"Androva was the older of the two worlds," continued Iona, "with a very established and long-standing society. The use of magic on Androva was carefully regulated by a set of rules known as the Code, and harmful and dangerous spells were not permitted.

"All Androvan magicians followed a training programme. This ensured that the rules were completely understood and accepted by everyone by the time they came of age. Violations of the Code were rare, and were quickly remedied.

"Life on Androva was slow to change, but most were happy with this, enjoying the security and predictability of their lives. Those seeking more excitement were encouraged to work in the Council's Foundation for Research, where the boundaries of magic were put to the test. Every day the Foundation tried to create the impossible. Things like being in two places at once. Or travelling to other faraway worlds. Or even eternal life.

"The aim of the Foundation was to be the first to discover new spells so that the use of these spells could then be controlled by the Council. As most of you will be aware, this Foundation no longer exists. There is a very good reason for that, which will become obvious later in the story."

Jax liked the sound of the Foundation very much. Imagine if it were your job every day to experiment with spells? It sounded brilliant. Revus watched his son, half proud, half exasperated. He could guess exactly what Jax was thinking.

"Terra was, therefore, the younger of the two worlds. It had no system for regulating its use of magic, and it supported progress at any cost. Progress meaning more powerful magicians, able to generate more wealth for Terra and improve the standard of living for the people of Terra. Life changed from year to year, with some of this progress turning out well and some of it not so well.

"There were elected representatives who attempted to control how the magic and its benefits were shared. But violations of their rules happened a lot.

"Magical power on Terra was obtained more by luck than anything else. Though there were some schools that underage magicians could attend if they wished, this was not compulsory. There was no consistency in the teaching. Despite all of this, Terra continued to grow and prosper, and most Terrans lived happily and without fear."

Jax and Darius both glanced at Shannon, wanting to see what she would make of this mixed description of her world. But Shannon was unconcerned. She thought that Iona's portrayal was fair, and she recognised a lot in what Iona said that was still true about Terra today.

"One day, Androva's Foundation for Research discovered how to create a portal between Androva and other worlds. This was a really exciting development and for a time the Council allowed the Foundation to experiment with different destinations and freely explore these other worlds. It was learned that some younger worlds had not even discovered magic yet, while others were only just starting to use it.

"Out of all the worlds, Androva was by far the most advanced in its use of magic. Unfortunately, this made the magicians who travelled through the portals less careful than they should have been." Iona stopped for a moment and clasped her hands together in her lap, her expression becoming more serious.

"Not enough safeguards were taken. The portals were not always closed properly. In the early days of portal creation, it was quite difficult to get the portal to open and stay open. The spellstations that we use today make everything more stable and predictable. But for the magicians at the Foundation, it was sometimes easier to leave a portal open rather than close it and have to go to all the trouble of getting it to open again the next time.

"It was a Terran magician by the name of Angelus who discovered an open portal between Terra and Androva. Before I continue, it is important you realise that Angelus did not start out as a bad magician. Each of us begins with the potential for good and bad, but it's the choices we make that decide who we become.

"According to later reports, he was ambitious, and quite gifted, though he had an unfortunate tendency towards occasional selfishness. He was not quite in his nineteenth year when he discovered the portal."

There was silence as the younger members of Iona's audience considered what she had said. But no one said anything, or asked any questions. They all wanted to hear what happened next.

Iona carried on.

"Angelus remained undetected by the magicians at the Foundation. He watched as one of the Androvan magicians stepped into the portal. Then he used his recently learned skill with an Invisibility Spell to conceal himself as he followed. Imagine the possibilities for a magician like Angelus at the Foundation. He possessed enormous natural talent, he was bound to follow no rules or authority, and he now had access to the most advanced spells on Androva."

Iona's words created a very powerful picture. Shannon, Jax, and Darius could all agree that it sounded like a complete and utter nightmare. Absolute power with no responsibility? It didn't get much worse than that.

"I don't suppose there's any chance this Angelus person decided to be sensible?" asked Darius hopefully. "I mean, he could have just stolen a couple of spells, returned to Terra to show them off, and left it at that," he suggested.

Even as he was saying it, he knew it wasn't true, but he wasn't quite ready for the story to continue yet. Jax looked at him sympathetically. Darius always hated to believe the worst about people. He had even trusted Marcus during his interrogation.

Shannon, on the other hand, could see exactly where the story was going, and it didn't look like

Terra was going to come out of it well. Even though she knew she was not responsible for what had happened all those years ago, she still felt guilty by association.

Jax nudged her, guessing what she was thinking. "Both sides were to blame," he pointed out. "Without the open portal, there would have been no opportunity for Angelus."

"Angelus did not behave with honour," Iona said. Shannon winced. This was obviously going to be bad. "He remained in the Foundation for many days as a silent observer, learning all its secrets. We know that he came close to discovery on two occasions. In order to remain undetected, he used magic to kill the two Foundation magicians who would otherwise have found him out."

"What?" gasped Shannon, voicing what Jax and Darius were also thinking. "How? I didn't know there was a spell that could do that!"

"There was not, there *is* not, at least not a spell that has been used by anyone else. Angelus had been getting close to the experiments being conducted to create a spell for eternal life. He simply reversed the steps of that spell, and it proved very effective.

"It left no sign, no trace on its victims. It wasn't until Angelus used the spell again later, to devastating effect, that they realised what it was.

And they understood that the first two Foundation magicians to die had also been subjected to it. In time it simply became known as the Death Spell."

No one spoke as the horror of Iona's words sunk in.

"The days continued to pass until Angelus was ready to make his move. At first it was thought that the two magicians had died from natural causes. But eventually other magicians working at the Foundation began to notice missing spells and other strange happenings that could not be explained away. Angelus must have known that he would soon be discovered. But by then, he did not care. He had increased his magical ability tenfold with all that he had learned from the Foundation. He also had spells at his disposal that were incredibly dangerous."

Iona stopped for a moment, as if she did not want to recall what happened next.

"What did he do?" asked Jax.

17 The Evil (Part Two)

"Angelus wanted to rule Androva. He was fed up with living in the shadows as an invisible presence. He wanted the magicians on this older world to know his name, to fear him and to do his bidding. He decided that the way to achieve this was by a demonstration of his strength.

"This demonstration..." Iona swallowed, "cost the lives of many innocent Androvans. He showed no mercy..." Her voice broke, and she stopped talking for a moment. No matter how many times she told the story, she always struggled at that part. Her blonde hair fell forward as she bowed her head to control her emotions so that she could carry on.

"They were not prepared," she managed to continue. "There was no resistance, but still he went on killing. After he had got rid of all the Foundation magicians, the Council members and their families were the next to die. Then any magician who showed any strength or defiance, until before long our society was broken.

"It took months before any defence could be organised, and those early attempts failed completely. It's hard for us to know exactly what it must have been like to live in those days. When everyone lived in dread of what Angelus would do next, and there was nothing except the terror. All hope was very nearly gone."

She looked at Revus, who pressed his lips together. Council records contained more information about exactly what Angelus had done and Revus had no intention of sharing any of it.

"But then Angelus decided that it wasn't enough to be the ruler of Androva. He wanted to rule his home world of Terra as well. And this gave us some possibility of fighting back. For Terra was a much bigger world with less organisation, and less order.

"On Androva, by destroying the Council, Angelus had destroyed the heart of our world. But on Terra it was more difficult for him to strike such a devastating blow. It took longer for him to build up the same fear and obedience on Terra."

Shannon almost sighed with relief. At least her world had made it difficult for Angelus. It wasn't much, but it was better than nothing.

"Angelus enlisted the help of his younger brother, Sandro. Yes, I know that you, Jax, and you, Darius, recognise that name. You will understand why when I have finished the story.

"Angelus shared some of his new, dangerous spells with his brother, to enable Sandro to speed up the conquering of Terra. But unfortunately for Angelus, and very fortunately for our two worlds, Sandro did not support what his brother was doing. He started a secret rebellion.

"It took Sandro weeks and weeks to gather enough support to challenge Angelus. Many had lost their courage in the face of what Angelus had done, and at first Sandro could find almost no one to stand alongside him.

"He was incredibly brave to continue, knowing that he could have been found out at any time. He persevered, and the turning point was when Sandro discovered a way to harvest the living magic on Terra. He was the first magic-taker."

Jax looked at Darius. It was strange hearing about the inventor of the spell that defined the way they lived.

"With this new skill, Sandro was able to convince more magicians on both Terra and Androva that they had a chance of beating Angelus. Gradually they gathered a large stockpile of harvested magic, and Sandro carried it to Androva one piece at a time.

"He was the only magician apart from Angelus who was permitted to travel freely between the two worlds. Before being stored, each piece of magic was filled with the Spell of Immobility. Sandro intended to create a cage of magic energy and somehow capture Angelus inside it."

Shannon felt her stomach churn. A magical cage. Made out of harvested magic. The quota. Surely this didn't mean...?

Iona continued. "By this time, Angelus had built a tower for himself out of the foundations of the old Council building. It was located on the mountain you can see some distance from Landor. From this stronghold he could see for miles around, and so he was satisfied that even if the frightened Androvans were to launch an attack, he would see it coming.

"Sandro decided to hide the harvested magic at the base of the tower. He covered one of the unused rooms in Protection Spells to keep the magic contained. He believed that Angelus would not suspect him, because who would be crazy enough to challenge Angelus in his own tower?"

Shannon, Jax, and Darius were leaning forward in their seats, spellbound by the story. Shannon remembered the mountain she had seen from the window in Jax's room, and guessed that this was what Iona was talking about. She shivered. She had not paid much attention to it at the time, but she could recall how dark and threatening it was.

"Eventually Sandro believed that he had enough harvested magic to contain Angelus. He contacted all of the other magicians who were a part of the rebellion and told them that he would make his move on the last day of the calendar month. That day came. When night fell, he suggested to Angelus that they visit the base of the tower, because he, Sandro, had acquired a gift for Angelus."

Iona now leaned forward herself, to make sure that her next words would be fully understood.

"By now, Angelus was nothing like the young magician he had been. All the good in him had been destroyed. You also have to understand what happens to you when you use your magic to take the life of another. You will never know peace again.

"The white glow of your magic gradually turns black, announcing your guilt to anyone who sees it. And every time you project a spell, you will feel the bitter taste of what you have done as the blackness pours through you. So it was for Angelus.

"On Androva, it had been hundreds of years since such a thing had been seen, but the historic records contained a handful of accounts describing this black transformation. Of course, those long-ago magicians did not use anything as awful as this Death Spell that Angelus had created. But they knew that using magic for such an evil purpose would turn it black.

"Perhaps Angelus did not care if he never knew peace again. But imagine what it is like. It becomes unbearable even to exist. Your mind is always fighting to get away from the blackness, but you cannot escape it. It follows you everywhere because it is part of you.

"So Angelus would always be unsatisfied. He could never be reasoned with. His evil acts would continue in a never-ending spiral of destruction."

Jax, Shannon, and Darius were horrified by Iona's words. It was as if they were in the middle of a bad dream, but they couldn't wake up to escape it, because they were already awake. It even seemed as if the room they were sitting in was getting darker.

Satisfied that they appreciated the significance of what she was describing, Iona began to speak again.

"Angelus followed Sandro to the base of the tower. He did not suspect his brother, confident as he was in his superior abilities. They reached the room, and Sandro unlocked it. He stepped aside so that Angelus could open the door and enter. Angelus started to open the door, then hesitated. He could probably feel the force of the magic within.

"There was so much harvested magic by now that even Sandro's Protection Spells were struggling to hold it back. Angelus began to close the door again, turning back to his brother to ask him to explain.

"Sandro, seeing his chance slipping away, gave Angelus a great push forwards in the centre of his chest. The door swung open, and Angelus staggered into the room. As he fell backwards and the magic enclosed him, he realised what was happening, and he gave a bellow of rage.

"But the magic was too powerful, even for him, and the combined Spells of Immobility slowly did their work. Sadly, the spells did not work quite fast enough for Sandro. Angelus's last act before being frozen was to project the Death Spell onto his brother."

"No!" said Shannon and Jax together. Darius looked too stunned to speak.

"I'm afraid so," said Iona unhappily. "He survived a few moments, just long enough to explain what had happened to him. He was found by two magicians in the tower who had heard the angry shout of Angelus, which by all accounts was loud enough to echo round the mountain.

"With Angelus contained, both worlds elected a new Council of leaders and the treaty was eventually agreed upon. To make sure that we never forget what Sandro did for us all, the mountain was from then on known as Sandro's Mountain."

Shannon nodded her head. So this was why Jax and Darius would have known Sandro's name. It was a fitting way to honour his bravery.

But Iona was not finished yet. "There is more," she went on. "During the treaty discussions, it became apparent that Angelus was fighting the magic in the Containment Room. Cracks had started to appear in the light that surrounded him. They realised it would need to be constantly maintained if they were going to keep Angelus frozen. And so the harvest quota was agreed upon.

"It was the requirement for the harvest quota that resulted in Terra losing its magicians. We had to preserve all available magic for the fight against Angelus. And more importantly we had to make sure that Terra never again created such a monster.

"Even on Androva, precautions were taken. The Foundation for Research was not rebuilt. You will remember me mentioning that storybooks are not permitted here, to make sure that no underage magicians are encouraged to dream of a different life.

"And the coming of age ceremony now includes a spell that fixes your magic ability from that moment onwards. This is to prevent any one magician from becoming more powerful than their natural ability will allow them to be."

Jax was now feeling quite terrible about having broken the Code so lightly. All of this pain and suffering, when compared to his teenage impatience with the rules, made him look like a total idiot. If I had known, he thought wretchedly, I would never have done it.

Shannon looked at him, understanding how he was feeling. "Remember, we did this together," she whispered to him. Shannon herself was now a bit worried about the magic she had harvested in the woodland the day before. She had obviously increased her powers of magic far beyond what Iona had called her "natural ability." But I'm not going to turn into another Angelus, she reassured herself.

Iona's story was drawing to a close. "Magic-taking has continued to this day," she said. "Each piece of harvested magic is always filled with the Spell of Immobility. The Containment Room in Sandro's Mountain is still there, though the tower has long since been destroyed. And the quota of magic required to keep Angelus contained has not changed.

"The magic inside the Containment Room is worn away from the inside, and replaced by us from the outside. We know that this is still happening, because the total size of the light inside that room never increases."

"How is that possible?" asked Jax. "All of this happened hundreds of years ago!"

"We don't know for sure," answered Iona. "Maybe the Spells of Immobility protect him from getting any older. Or maybe he had already discovered how to complete the spell they were working on in the Foundation that could give him eternal life."

"Now you understand," said Revus wearily. He had been leaning against the wall, and now he stood up straight again. "The quota is falling short, and it is only a matter of time before Angelus escapes. We don't know how quickly it will happen, but we have to expect the worst. We must come up with a plan before it is too late. The prophecy says that you"—he looked at Jax and Darius—"and you"—he looked at Shannon—"are the ones to decide what happens." At this, he waited for a moment, but no-one else spoke.

"I still cannot see how three underage magicians can defeat the greatest Evil that our two worlds have ever known. I have to report back to the rest of the Council in the morning, and at the moment I have no good news to tell them."

18 The Interrogation

"I don't understand something," began Shannon hesitantly. "Why have you never carried out the Spell of Removal on Angelus? Surely once he was held by the Spell of Immobility, you could have taken away his magic and then everything would have been OK?"

Revus sighed with irritation. This was his second sleepless night in a row, and despite his well-known self-control, his impatience to start the interrogation was starting to get the better of him. He gave Shannon an annoyed glance, and she immediately regretted asking the question.

"No, Father," said Jax, looking at Revus unsmilingly. "Do not allow your impatience to cloud your judgement. She knows little of our world. Wouldn't you think her foolish if she had *not* asked that question?"

Revus looked at his son in astonishment. Then, grudgingly, he admitted the truth of what

Jax was saying. He began to feel a new respect for his son.

He sat down. "You are correct, Jax. I apologise, Shannon," he said, turning to her. "Allow me to explain. The Spell of Removal is not an attacking spell. It is a matter of honour. It cannot be carried out on a magician who is being held against his or her will by another spell.

"Here we are accustomed to abiding by the decisions of the Council. A magician would bring dishonour on his or her family if they contested the Council's decision and refused their punishment." On hearing this, Shannon looked at Jax, understanding why he had not fought against Marcus at the Assembly. He had certainly behaved with honour, she thought.

"Therefore," concluded Revus, "it was never possible to carry out the Spell of Removal on Angelus. He would obviously not have consented to it, but more than that, his power was so great that no one could catch him unawares.

"We don't know if anyone tried it, but we do of course know that if they did, they were unsuccessful. Every magician who tried to attack Angelus paid for it with his life. And once he was captured by Sandro in the giant Spell of Immobility, we could not carry out the Spell of Removal then either."

Shannon understood. "Thank you for

explaining," she said to Revus, and he inclined his head, replying "You are very welcome."

"Now," said Revus, "we must start the interrogation. The night is already half gone. Usually I would take you back to the Council examination rooms to conduct my questioning, but I believe that you are all more likely to tell me what I need to know if we remain here. The Council rooms are a bit more... uninviting, shall we say?"

Jax and Darius could bear out the truth of this statement. Their interrogations by Marcus had been carried out in rooms that were much less welcoming than Darius's house.

Shannon found herself feeling more and more nervous now that Revus had mentioned the interrogation again. It sounded quite scary. Seeing her anxious expression, Revus decided that things were more likely to go well if Shannon knew what to expect from the interrogation. He gave her a brief explanation.

"An interrogation by a Council member is simply a structured question and answer session. I will ask the questions, and you will provide the answers. If I believe at any time that you are not being truthful, or that you are holding back in the information you provide, I can use certain spells to encourage you. I will adjust these spells according to how I think you will respond to them.

"If I think you need to be frightened into telling me what I need to know, then I can make you feel very scared. On the other hand, if I think your fear is holding you back, I can make you feel as if everything is great and that talking to me is the best idea you ever had."

Shannon didn't like the idea of having her emotions manipulated. But she accepted that the Council had to use something on magicians who would not co-operate. "Is that it though?" she asked. "What happens if the person you're interrogating resists the spells?"

She turned to Jax, adding, "Jax obviously did resist his interrogation, so it must be possible."

Revus nodded. "It is possible to resist, though it takes a great deal of effort and magical skill." He glanced at his son and half laughed. "This is a strange situation. Jax did most definitely show great ability in resisting his interrogation. But this can't be seen as a good thing because of the circumstances.

"There is one final spell that is allowed to be used as a last resort. It is very aggressive, but its use is not permitted in underage magicians, so you do not need to worry about it. Now let us begin."

Iona half rose from her chair, as if she were going to leave the room, but Revus asked her to stay. He started his questioning almost gently, asking about the first daylight visit that Jax and Darius had made to Terra, a little over one week before. This time both boys admitted that Shannon had seen them, though Jax did not volunteer any more information than that.

Revus waited for a moment, and then in the same pleasant tone, he offered to use a spell to help them remember. Jax looked defiant for a moment, then relented. He supposed there was little point hiding anything now. He told Revus about his Sygnus activation and the belief he'd had even then that Shannon was a magician.

Revus asked Shannon to describe the same events from her point of view. He also covered what had happened to her in the week afterwards, frowning as she explained how her magic abilities had gradually revealed themselves. "You are sure this happened during just one week?" he asked.

"Yes…" said Shannon uncertainly. "Is that bad?"

"It is fast," answered Revus, still frowning. "It is very fast."

Next, Revus turned his attention back to Jax, and asked him to relate what had happened when he had returned to visit Shannon. When Jax reached the part about Shannon's Solo Transference spell, Revus stopped him, looking a little annoyed. "There is no need for embellishment. You will not succeed in distracting me by making up ridiculous stories. I am only interested in the truth."

"This is the truth," said Jax, equally annoyed. "If I were going to distract you, Father, I would be a bit more subtle than that. Besides, you saw what she did to Marcus earlier, you should not doubt her ability."

Revus looked at Shannon for a moment, and self-consciously she lowered her gaze. "It is possible that what you did in the Assembly was a one-time thing that you can't repeat," he said to her. "That really is the most likely explanation. There is no logical way to account for someone of your age and very limited experience being able to hold the Council's most powerful magician in such a spell. There is a high chance you won't be able to do it again."

Jax pushed his chair back slightly, really angry now. "Go on, show him!" he said to Shannon, raising his voice. "Show him that it was not a one-time thing!" Shannon looked across at Revus, nervous about how he would react to Jax's words.

"Don't put the poor girl on the spot in this way," Revus responded calmly. "And it is not necessary to shout. You cannot expect her to be able to project a spell in the middle of her first interrogation. Such a thing would be ridiculous," he finished dismissively.

Oh, would it? Shannon thought to herself, feeling irritated. At first she had been too intimidated by Revus to contradict him when he had explained to her that she wouldn't be able to repeat what she had done in the Assembly. But she wasn't happy about being called a "poor girl." Or about the way Revus had just spoken to Jax.

"Why?" she challenged Revus with a glare. "Why would such a thing be ridiculous?"

Revus, realising that Darius was also looking infuriated on behalf of his friends, decided to project a Harmony Spell to regain control of the situation. He lowered his hands until they were out of sight, under the table that the meal had been served on. Then he projected the glow of the spell. The glow was gentle in appearance, but very effective.

It reached Darius first. He immediately calmed down and then looked uncertainly at Revus, not sure why he had been so annoyed a moment before. Then Jax felt himself start to relax. He gritted his teeth together, realising that this was the work of a spell from his father, but he could not maintain the intensity of his former anger.

It is always harder to resist a spell when you don't see it coming. When Jax had faced Marcus in the interrogation room, he had been alert for any spell Marcus sent in his direction. But this time Revus had taken him by surprise.

Finally the spell reached Shannon. She could feel it on her skin, like a soft, slightly warm, silver mist. But although she looked at it curiously for a moment, it did not dissolve her anger. In fact, once she noticed what was happening to Darius and Jax, and she realised what the spell was, her anger grew. How dare he try to control our emotions? she thought indignantly.

Before she could change her mind, she lifted her hands. "No," she said to Revus in a clear voice. "Don't do that." And she used the Spell of Immobility to freeze the glow coming from Revus. She did not throw all her magic into the spell the way she had in the Assembly. She measured it out, until it was just enough to stop the glow of the Harmony Spell and no more.

Revus at first reacted just as Marcus had done, and tried to push the spell outwards again. Shannon shook her head. "Please take back the spell," she said. "If you don't, I will just have to do it for you."

Revus looked incredulous. "You cannot do this!" he said. Shannon pushed her spell further outwards, and feeling the immobility travelling past his hands and into his body, Revus tried again. "You *will not* do this!"

Shannon responded by pushing the spell right

back into his head, until he was unable to speak. She held it there for a moment, to make sure he understood what was happening, and then released him.

"I am sorry," she said. Her cheeks were a bit pink, but her voice remained clear and strong. "If you are going to get the truth out of this interrogation, you will have to listen to us. Don't wash away our anger. We are being honest with you, so please be honest with us."

Revus sat as if turned to stone, unable to believe what had just happened. Iona was the first to break the shocked silence. "Revus, now do you see? Do you see that the prophecy could be true?"

Revus eventually spoke. "I don't know exactly what is going on here, but I promise to take your responses entirely seriously from now on," he said in a low voice. "No matter how unbelievable they seem. I am sorry for doubting you," he said, facing Shannon. Then he turned to Jax and Darius. "I am sorry for doubting all of you. It won't happen again."

Gathering himself together, Revus returned to the interrogation. Soon he had learned all about their plan to break into the restricted section of the Repository of Records, and the lessons that Jax had given Shannon to prepare her. Revus was particularly interested in the methods Shannon had used to escape the Containment Spell.

When they described finding the treaty and their horror at realising what they had done, Revus could see they were telling the truth. He shook his head sadly. "You should now understand that even the best intentions can lead to disaster. You intended to find the treaty so that you could understand the consequences of what you had done and figure out how to fix them, which is a good intention. But you actually made things worse.

"However, this is a blame that must be shared. We intended to protect our underage magicians on Androva from the burden of knowledge that is the treaty, until the coming of age ceremony. A good intention, I think you will agree? But that created a situation where underage magicians were required to follow a set of rules with no explanation. Perhaps it was inevitable that those rules would one day be broken."

Revus then spent some time on the previous interrogations that Jax and Darius had experienced with Marcus. He did not comment when he heard exactly which methods Marcus had used. He also remained silent when Darius described the promise that Marcus had made to him—that Jax would be spared the Spell of Removal if Darius told Marcus everything.

But Revus's expression became gradually

much darker, and his mouth was set in a forbidding line. No one doubted that Revus would take this up with Marcus later.

Finally it was Shannon's turn to describe how she had increased her magic ability. Her audience was at first amazed and then became fearful at what she was describing. When Shannon had finished, Revus and Iona looked at her uneasily. Worried, she turned to Jax for reassurance, and he gave her a small smile, though he also looked quite shocked. "What is it?" Shannon finally asked. "Why are you all looking at me like that?"

Iona replied. "What you have done, Shannon, is incredibly dangerous. You were already showing great ability in such a short space of time. But now you have made yourself into an incredibly powerful magician, perhaps unbeatable. You have achieved this in a way that would not have been permitted on Androva. Just like Angelus did. The only difference between you is what you choose to do with that power."

19 Waiting For The Council To Decide

Shannon was horrified. "You can't compare me with that... that monster!" she cried. Then her face fell, as she remembered that earlier, while Iona was telling the story of Angelus, she had herself made the comparison in her own mind. She had reassured herself that she was not going to turn into another Angelus. But how could she convince Revus and Iona?

She tried again, more calmly this time. "Look, I'm not even fourteen until next month. I'm not interested in world domination. I just want to help. That's all I've wanted to do, ever since I first learned about the consequences of breaking the Code." Everyone could hear the honesty in her quiet words, and the atmosphere in the room began to return to normal.

Jax and Darius nodded. "That's true," added

Jax earnestly. "Shannon has been the cautious one in all of this. I was the troublemaker, not her."

"Well, I'm sure that comes as a *huge* surprise to everyone," responded Revus, sighing irritably.

"I'll do anything you want to prove that I mean no harm," offered Shannon. "Isn't there a spell you can project to show that I'm telling the truth?"

Iona smiled at Shannon, her eyes kind. "It's not a matter of whether you are telling the truth right now, Shannon. We can all see that you are. It is more about what you may become in the future."

Iona looked at Revus, her eyebrows raised in a question. "With your permission, Revus, I think I should show them the Prophecy story, don't you? Almost one whole day has passed since I last looked at it, so some things may be clearer now."

Revus walked to the window and looked outside at the night sky, which was starting to become paler with the first light of dawn. He thought for a moment, then agreed. "Yes, I don't see why not. There is still a little time left."

Iona rested her elbows on the table, and Darius gestured to Shannon to sit back a bit. He hurriedly stacked the dishes and cups and moved them to one side.

"We need to leave the table clear," he

whispered to her. Very soon a glow appeared from Iona's hands and began to form into shapes on the table in front of her. Shannon watched closely, fascinated.

Soon she could recognise herself in one of the shapes, and Jax in another. Then she saw the Assembly and the Council again, followed by a portal room, the mountains, and then some kind of small underground chamber that she had never seen before.

There were three figures in the room, but she could not make them out clearly. The shapes began to move faster and faster, until she could no longer follow what was happening. Finally they disappeared.

Iona took a deep breath and leaned back again. Her eyes glinted with tears, and Shannon asked, "What's the matter?"

Iona did not answer at first. Then she started by saying, "Darius, you are no longer in the prophecy. Whatever your part in this was supposed to be, you have played it."

"But I can't just stop," protested Darius, though part of him was feeling a tiny bit relieved. "I still want to help."

Iona continued as if he had not spoken. "There will be an Assembly today, as we already know. The harvests of this night have failed to reach the quota for the month. Angelus can no longer be contained. The Council must decide on a plan of attack against Angelus.

"I can see the confrontation, which will take place before another full day and night has passed. There are two magicians standing against Angelus. One of them is you, Shannon. The other could be Jax, but that is not certain. I still cannot see who is victorious. I am also unable to see if everyone survives."

Iona reached for Darius and clasped his hand. "Your bravery is not in question, Darius," she reassured him softly. "But you cannot force yourself into a destiny that does not belong to you."

Shannon thought she was going to be sick. Jax could feel her trembling beside him, and he put his arm around her. Revus was resting his chin in his hand, frowning as he considered what Iona had said. Most of the prophecy was the same as he had heard from Iona at the start of the evening.

The difference this time was the certainty regarding when the confrontation against Angelus would take place. They had less time than he had hoped. Looking up, he noticed that Shannon was very pale and shaking with fright. He was suddenly reminded how young and inexperienced she was.

The average Terran girl of her age would not

normally expect to encounter anything like this outside of a storybook. His stern expression softened slightly.

"Do not doubt yourself," he told her. "You still have the same strength that you demonstrated to us before you saw the Prophecy story. Nothing has changed. You will not do this alone. The Council will not allow you or Jax to stand against Angelus without help, whatever the prophecy says." Iona looked as if she were about to say something in disagreement, but then changed her mind.

Shannon tried to be brave. You got yourself into this, she told herself. Now you have to deal with the consequences. She remembered for a moment the Monday morning in the school library when she had looked up consequences in the dictionary. It seemed like a million years ago.

Revus then spoke to Jax. "I know I can depend on you, Jax. Whatever our disagreements in the past, I have never questioned your courage. I will return as soon as the Assembly is over and tell you the plan. Please try to get some rest in the meantime."

"What about you, Father?" responded Jax. "When will you rest? You cannot go on forever without sleeping."

"I will be alright," said Revus firmly. "There are still a few hours before the Assembly starts, and once I have spoken to Marcus, I will return home to get some sleep."

"Why are you going to see Marcus?" asked Jax, narrowing his eyes suspiciously. "I told you the truth about my interrogation."

"I know that," said Revus. "It is because I believe what you have told me that I intend to raise it with Marcus." As he said this, he scowled. Then without saying anything further, he left the room.

Shannon, Jax, and Darius exchanged glances, not knowing what to do next. Shannon's sleeping pattern was so disrupted by now that she didn't know whether she was tired or not. She felt drained from everything she had seen and heard that night. But she knew she was too worried about everything just to go straight to sleep.

Iona realised that Marek would soon be arriving back from his job at the Repository of Magic, and that the news about the harvest quota would not be good. She suggested that the three friends take some food and drink from the kitchen and go to the training room. Most houses in Landor had a training room, though not all were as large and grand as the one in Jax's house.

"Why don't you play a game to take your mind off things for a while?" said Iona. "See if you can teach Shannon Time Trial or something."

At first Jax and Darius were slightly taken

aback at the thought of playing a game when there were so many more serious things going on. But they soon realised it didn't make sense to sit around worrying. There was nothing they could do until the Council had heard the information gathered by Revus.

Darius led the way to the back of the house and into the training room. Shannon recognised the same blue haze around the edges as she had seen before. After they had each eaten something, Shannon waited for the boys to explain the game to her.

"It's basically like an endurance test," started Darius. "You take an ordinary object, like this plate for example, and you have to use your magic to hold it in the air in front of you for as long as possible."

"That doesn't sound particularly difficult," replied Shannon in surprise.

"Ah, but that's not all," said Jax, grinning. "While you are trying to keep the plate steady, Darius and I get to use any spell we like to distract you. The only rule is that we can't cause you physical pain. But apart from that, anything goes," he finished, his grin getting bigger. "You can't fight the spells we throw at you. The point of the game is to keep the plate in the air. We all get a turn, and the one who holds the plate up the longest is the winner."

"It sounds great," said Shannon, smiling. "Can one of you go first so that I can see how it's done?"

"No," answered Jax. "You should go first. Given your now legendary magical ability, I think Darius and I need the element of surprise if we're going to stand any chance of winning!"

Shannon reluctantly agreed. Darius picked up the plate and held it in front of her until she had surrounded it with a glow that was strong enough to hold the plate on its own. There was a large wooden clock high up on the wall at one end of the room, and Jax called out the time, followed by "Go!"

At first, he and Darius circled Shannon, trying to figure out the best way to start. Darius began with a basic disorientation spell that made the room spin around Shannon, and just for a moment she wobbled on her feet, and the plate wobbled too. Jax followed up by creating a gale-force wind that nearly knocked Shannon off her feet. With a determined expression, she crouched down a bit and held on.

Then Darius made the floor underneath her appear as if it had turned to quicksand. Feeling her feet sinking, she glanced downwards, nearly dropping the plate. Finally Jax created a spell like a raincloud that hovered over Shannon for a moment, then drenched her. It was like having a bucket of icy cold water poured on her head, and she screamed, allowing the plate to fall.

All three were laughing as Jax and Darius congratulated Shannon on her time. She was amazed to realise that when the plate had finally fallen, each spell had immediately stopped and she was now completely dry again.

"Who's next?" she asked eagerly. She wanted to experience the game from the other side. Darius volunteered to go next. He knew that Jax wanted to go last so that he would know the time he had to beat. Once the plate was in the air again and the time had been called out, Jax started creating spells to distract Darius.

First he generated a heavy cloud to lay across Darius's shoulders, which made him bend over with the effort of resisting its weight. This was followed by a dark mist that covered Darius's eyes so that he could no longer see what he was doing. Shannon was still trying to think of something that she could do. She didn't know any of the more complicated spells that Jax and Darius could use. Suddenly she had an idea.

She began lifting Darius up, until in a short while he had travelled all the way to the ceiling. It was more difficult than doing the spell on herself, but using all her concentration, she managed it. Jax, giving her a quick grin of approval, waited until Darius was up as far as he could go, then removed the dark mist.

Seeing that he was up at the ceiling, Darius yelled in surprise, and the plate fell. Just as before, all the spells ended with the falling plate, and Darius returned to the ground.

"Pretty good going," congratulated Jax. "You nearly lasted as long as Shannon."

Then it was Jax's turn. He quickly created the glow that would hold the plate steady, and then he turned to Darius and Shannon expectantly. Darius called out the time, and he and Shannon began. Darius's first spell was to surround Jax in an icy blue cloud. It did not appear to have much of an effect at first, but as the time went on, Jax gradually began to shiver.

Meanwhile, Shannon was still wondering about what she could do to unsettle Jax and make him drop the plate. It couldn't be the same thing that she had done to Darius, because Jax might be expecting that. Finally, she thought of something.

Reaching into the pocket of her jeans, she pulled out the black pen that she had used to do her homework with Penny the previous day. She surrounded it with magic, and set it to work on Jax. The pen began to draw on his face. First it drew a pair of glasses around his eyes, and then it gave him a moustache above his mouth. After that, it drew a love heart on his cheek.

By this time, Darius was giggling so much that

he had collapsed on the floor, and Shannon was laughing so hard she could only just keep the spell going.

Jax looked outraged, and wasn't finding it funny at all. Though his teeth were chattering with cold from Darius's ice cloud, he was still keeping the plate in the air.

Eventually Darius recovered enough to try one more thing. He turned the floor underneath Jax to a sheet of ice. Jax's feet slid from under him, and he couldn't keep his balance. He landed in an undignified heap, laughing as the plate fell and the spells stopped.

Jax was declared the winner, and the three friends continued laughing for several minutes. Iona's suggestion of playing a game to stop them thinking about the night ahead had worked very well. They succeeded in keeping their smiles as they went upstairs to try to get some rest, and managed to fall asleep without too much difficulty. The afternoon was drawing to a close when Iona came to wake them up.

"The Council Assembly is over," she told them. "They have made their decision."

20 The Decision

Shannon, Jax, and Darius heard Iona's words with a feeling of dread. Shannon was the worst affected, and fear made her brown eyes huge in her pale face. All three used a quick Cleaning Spell, and were about to follow Iona downstairs, when she drew Jax to one side.

"I must warn you," she whispered to him urgently. "I have looked at the Prophecy story again, and there is now a dark cloud over the events of this evening. It is essential to the future of both Androva and Terra that Shannon is part of our defence against Angelus. You must do all that you can to protect us."

Shannon and Darius, waiting for Jax, both wondered what Iona was saying to him. He was obviously alarmed, if his expression was anything to go by. Shannon intended to ask him what was going on, but Iona did not give her the chance. As soon as she had finished talking to Jax, she said, "Quickly now!" and almost pushed the three of them downstairs.

Revus was waiting for them. "I hope you got some rest?" he asked them. "We have no time to lose. Please come with me to the Council offices right away," he requested, looking at Jax and Shannon. Then he turned away to open the front door.

Darius made to follow Revus as well, but Iona stopped him. "No," she said quietly. "This is not your fight, Darius. You must say goodbye to your friends and wait with the rest of us to find out what happens tonight."

Shannon gave Darius a hug, and he whispered, "Good luck." Jax and Darius exchanged a half-smile, and Darius said, "You're my best friend. I wish I could stand beside you."

Jax nodded. "Thank you," he said in a low voice. Then he and Shannon turned to follow Revus into the late afternoon sunlight. Darius watched them go, his face downcast.

The walk back to the Council building seemed to go faster this time. Shannon was finding it hard to think about anything except how scared she was. She couldn't ask Jax what Iona had said to him, not when Revus was right there.

She was only vaguely aware of the buildings and people they passed. Jax walked closely alongside her, their shoulders sometimes touching, but he did not say anything. Occasionally their eyes met, and his smile reassured her a little.

Soon Revus was opening the heavy doors to the Council offices. Shannon noticed that the silver embellishments on the wood glinted in the slanting rays of the sun. Then they were inside, and it was much darker. There were several custodians in the hallway, and all conversation stopped as Jax and Shannon walked forward.

Jax leaned in to whisper to Shannon. "It must be because we're the greatest underage magicians the world has ever seen," he said, and was rewarded with a small smile in return.

Revus beckoned them forward, and they entered a corridor. Before long Revus was opening the door called Council Examination Rooms, and next the Assembly room door. The room was quiet, as if everyone seated behind the long desk were waiting for their arrival.

Jax scanned the faces, quickly realising that Marcus was missing and that another magician had taken his place. He turned to his father, and Revus guessed what Jax was going to ask. "Marcus has agreed that he would best serve Androva in an alternative role from now on," he said quietly. Jax raised his eyebrows in surprise. He wished he knew what had happened between Revus and Marcus earlier that day. Revus must have said some pretty serious things to get Marcus to resign his place on the Council.

Revus cleared his throat. "Friends," he began, addressing the seated Council. "Here are the two underage magicians mentioned by the prophecy. You will of course recognise my son and the girl from our Assembly yesterday. Now that we are in possession of all the facts and have concluded our debate, I have brought them here so that they can be told what the Council has decided."

Jax and Shannon looked at each other, wondering what they would hear next. Jax was standing very straight and tall, and Shannon copied him. She decided that she would try to conquer her fear, at least for the moment. If Jax can do it, then so can I, she reasoned. Jax himself was actually feeling almost as nervous as Shannon, but he was determined not to show it.

Revus continued, "We are all agreed that the prophecy should be taken into consideration. But we also agree that it makes no sense to allow two underage magicians to face this Evil. There are better plans of attack that we can follow using experienced magicians, and it is one of these plans that has been decided upon today.

"Despite the exceptional magical ability of the girl, we have decided that she will not fight. Her ability is judged to be a danger to our world and her own."

Shannon and Jax could not hide their shock at hearing this. But Revus was not finished yet.

"And so, once we have fought and defeated Angelus this night, it is the decision of the Council that the Spell of Removal be carried out on the girl immediately."

Shannon gasped. "*What?*" said Jax to his father in disbelief. "I think I must have misheard you. You want to carry out the Spell of Removal on *Shannon?*"

"It is the only logical decision," Revus replied. Though he felt sorry for his son, he kept his expression firm. "We believe that we have a high chance of success with our plan to defeat Angelus, and we will not expose either of you to the risk of joining the fight. Particularly Shannon. It is the least we can do for the Terran family to whom she belongs. And it is only right that we remove her magical ability before we return her to Terra. We must make some amends for having broken the terms of the treaty.

"We have calculated how long it will take before Angelus is free of the Spell of Immobility that restrains him, and it will not be before midnight. By then we will have a team of magicians in place to prevent his escape. The final step will be the Spell of Removal. For both of them."

Jax took a step backwards, horrified by his

father's explanation. "This is wrong," he managed, shaking his head. "Shannon's ability is the only chance we have of defeating this... this *thing* that is trapped in the mountain. And you have no right to remove it." He grabbed Shannon's hand, as if to run out of the room with her.

Revus, who had half expected such a reaction, immediately projected a Containment Spell towards his son. Taking no chances, he made it very quick and extremely forceful. Jax let out a small cry and fell to the floor. Revus had guessed that Shannon would not try to run away without Jax, and he was right. Shannon crouched down to find out if Jax was OK, and saw that he had fainted from the pain. Looking up at Revus with angry eyes, she was about to fight back, when he shook his head and began speaking.

"Do not be foolish. You cannot fight the entire Council, no matter how great your abilities. Twenty versus one is too many, even for you. And if you make an attempt, Jax will suffer for it."

Shannon looked over her shoulder at the other Council members, some of whom were already standing up to defend themselves. She turned back to Revus and said to him fiercely, "How *could* you? He is your son, how can you do this to him? I thought you were on our side!"

"We are on the same side," answered Revus calmly. "We all want what is best for Androva and Terra, not what is best for ourselves as individuals. Now you will accompany me to one of the interrogation rooms. If you try to escape, you will both be punished. I'm sure you would not wish Jax to suffer the Spell of Removal? You may choose to resist, but he will not. So you see it is best for everyone if you do as you are told."

Jax was starting to come round, and he groaned as he became aware of the pain of the containment band in his head. Revus pulled him up onto his feet, and, supporting Jax under his shoulders, he took him out of the room. The only sound was the dragging of Jax's black boots on the stone floor.

Miserably, Shannon followed Revus out of the Assembly and into one of the interrogation rooms. Revus put Jax in one of the two plain wooden chairs, where he slumped down, still not properly alert. Then Revus brought them some water and a plate of food, and closed the door.

Shannon looked around the room, seeing that all of the walls were made from the same smooth stone, and that there was only one window, high up and out of reach. The only way out of this room will be the door, she thought. She sat down beside Jax, reaching to smooth his hair back from his forehead.

"Are you OK?" she whispered. "Try to relax, don't fight the spell."

After a short while, Jax half opened his eyes. He looked awful. The pain had made his face appear grey, and his forehead had a sheen of perspiration on it. "Just... give me a minute," he managed. Closing his eyes again, he breathed in and began to work on escaping the spell. Fairly soon, the agonising pressure of the band was reduced to a more bearable level, as he suppressed his magic beneath it. Then he stopped.

"I dare not escape the spell completely," he said to Shannon. "If I do, he will probably just come closer again and restore it to how it was before. And at least this way, we will know if he travels any distance away from this room, because the spell will disappear."

"OK," Shannon replied. "Anything is an improvement to you being unconscious from the pain," she added shakily.

"What happened after I passed out?" asked Jax, sitting up a bit straighter in the chair. These things haven't become any more comfortable since I was last here facing Marcus, he thought.

Shannon lowered her head, not wanting to answer. "You have to tell me," he persisted, lifting her chin so that she was forced to meet his gaze. "We need to come up with a plan to get out of here, so I have to know everything."

Shannon realised the truth of what Jax was saying. So she told him. His face looked like a thundercloud when she had finished. Then he winced. He was so angry he had forgotten about suppressing his magic under the containment band for a moment, and the renewed pressure really hurt.

"I need to tell you something too," he said, and proceeded to enlighten her about the warning Iona had given him earlier.

"What are we going to do?" he continued, getting up out of the chair and pacing the room. "I don't want to make things any worse than they already are, but I really do believe that my father has got it wrong. The Council are obviously scared of what you might turn into if they allow you to be the one to defeat Angelus. Maybe they think you'll be invincible."

He paused for a moment. "It is possible to be powerful *and* good. Recommending the Spell of Removal just because of something that might happen is crazy. You may as well allow fear to dictate all of your decisions and have done with it. But what kind of life is that?"

He stopped pacing and stood in front of Shannon. "You know what we have to do. We have to escape this building, go to Sandro's Mountain, and fight Angelus. We just need to figure out how to escape, and how to win the fight."

"Oh, when you put it like that, I don't know why I was so worried," replied Shannon trying to laugh and not quite succeeding. "Just those two little things to figure out, and then we'll be fine!"

"We will be," said Jax firmly, taking both of her hands in his. "We'll be fine. We will wait for nightfall and then make our escape."

21 The Mountain

The time seemed to pass very slowly as Jax and Shannon waited for the sky outside the window to turn dark. They discussed their ideas about how to escape, and eventually settled on using a Deceiving Spell, which they would both project at the same time.

Jax reasoned that it had worked perfectly well at the Repository of Records two nights ago, and this time they would both be projecting the spell, which would make it even stronger. Not to mention that Shannon was more powerful now. "My father was probably expecting that the fear of punishment would stop us from escaping," said Jax scornfully. "He should realise that doesn't work by now."

There was a pause, and then Shannon asked tentatively, "What happened to your mother?"

Jax shrugged as if he didn't care, but Shannon knew him well enough by now to know that he did care. "She died when I was three years old," he replied. "Some kind of sudden illness. My father doesn't like to talk about it."

"I'm sorry," said Shannon softly. He gave her a grateful smile, but did not offer any more information, so she decided to change the subject.

"We have to make it to the mountain well before midnight if we're going to get there before the Council and their grand plan," said Shannon. "But how can we? The mountain looked very far away when I saw it from your window."

"I've been thinking about that," answered Jax, glad that he had the answer to at least one of their questions. "There must be a portal room in the Repository of Magic building that has the exact coordinates for the mountain.

"How else would they be able to transport the harvested magic to where Angelus is being held captive? They couldn't carry it all that way—it would be nearly all gone by the time they arrived."

"Of course!" said Shannon, relieved. "I should have realised that portals weren't just for travelling between worlds. How far away are we from the Repository of Magic building though?"

"It's not far," said Jax. "Landor is not a big city, and the Council built most of the main buildings fairly close together for convenience.

I've been to the Repository of Magic so many times, I could find my way blindfolded."

Then he frowned. Putting his hands in his pockets, he kicked at the chair leg. "All of this is great, but it doesn't help us figure out how we are going to beat him. We can't exactly carry out a Death Spell..."

"No, of course not!" interrupted Shannon, shocked. "I thought we would just try to hold him with the Spell of Immobility until the more experienced magicians arrive."

"And then what?" pressed Jax. "You know that they can't do anything to him while he's being held by the Spell of Immobility. My father said they would carry out the Spell of Removal, but how can they? I wish I knew exactly what their plan was. There just doesn't seem any way to make it work."

Shannon hesitated, then asked, "Do you know how to do the Spell of Removal?"

"Me?" asked Jax, astonished.

"Yes, you," confirmed Shannon, looking thoughtful. "I've been wondering... What if I use the Spell of Immobility on him, then we agree on a signal between us. On that signal, I immediately drop my spell, and you immediately project the Spell of Removal!" she finished, looking hopeful. "What do you think? If we took him completely by surprise, might it work?"

Jax had at first started to shake his head, and then he stopped. "I don't know…" he began. "I've obviously never done the Spell of Removal. I know how it works in theory, but I'm not sure if that would be enough. It's not like I have any better ideas though. Let me think about it some more." He stopped talking and sat back down in the chair, resting his chin on his hands.

Shannon waited, staring at the walls and noticing that there was a crack in the stone to her left. She scuffed her trainers on the floor and let out a small sigh. Being stuck in one room was really boring.

She looked across at Jax, who was still deep in thought, his face scrunched up with concentration. Eventually, despite the uncomfortable chair, she felt herself falling asleep.

Jax was unable to come up with a better alternative to Shannon's idea. Turning to tell her, he realised that she was asleep. He looked at her for a moment, his face softening. He had known her for such a short space of time, and yet he couldn't imagine his life without her now.

I wish we could have met under different circumstances, he thought. Imagine if she had grown up in my world, and we'd just met at the Seminary of Magic or something. I bet we would have had a great time.

Suddenly he heard someone at the door, and he turned just in time to see it opening. He jumped up out of the chair as Shannon sleepily raised her head. Their visitor was a member of the Council. His name was Valena, and he was one of the younger magicians. He had blond hair, neatly combed, and eyes of a rather startling blue. Though his expression was calm, when he spoke it was quite forcefully.

"Jax," he began, "are you alright? Are you suffering any after-effects from the Containment Spell?"

"No," answered Jax uncertainly, thinking, Why are you here and what do you want?

"Good. And Shannon?" Valena continued, turning to check Shannon as well.

"I'm alright," replied Shannon, slightly suspicious. This man was obviously from the Council, and therefore it was very strange that he would be concerned about their well-being. She looked at Jax questioningly, but before he could say anything, Valena spoke again.

"I don't have much time, so I will make this quick," continued Valena. "You need to know that not all of the Council are in agreement with everything that is happening. The vote was evenly split, ten on each side, until Revus convinced Helena to vote in favour of his plan. Revus can be very persuasive when he wants to be.

"The point is that some of us think you should be allowed to fight. But everyone is so afraid. No one is completely certain what to do for the best. When someone like Revus is so sure of himself, it really influences the rest. But I think you deserve a chance.

"Not just because of the prophecy, but because of your bravery and your combined strength. So I will escort you from here to my own portal room, and give you the coordinates for Sandro's Mountain. After that, it's up to you."

Shannon and Jax looked at each other in excitement. "Really?" asked Jax, turning back to Valena doubtfully. "You would help us? You would go against the Council's decision and my father?"

"Yes," Valena replied simply. "There may not even be a Council after tonight. I am doing what I think is right for Androva. When the time comes, I will face my punishment without hesitation. Come, we must go. Revus will have departed by now to put his plan into motion."

Just as Valena said this, Jax realised that the Containment Spell was lifting. He sighed with relief. Then Valena left the interrogation room, and Jax and Shannon followed closely behind him. It was all very quiet outside in the corridor. There were two custodians out in the main entrance hall, but neither paid them any attention.

The streets outside were also silent in the gathering darkness. There was a strange feeling in the air, almost as if everyday life had been paused, and everyone was holding their breath. Waiting for some kind of sign before they could begin living again.

Valena's house was not far away, and though it was quite small, it was very welcoming inside. They descended immediately to the portal room, and Valena ushered Jax and Shannon through the door.

"The destination is set," he told them. "You just have to repeat the sequence. You will find yourselves at the end of an underground passageway, where you will see steps leading up to the surface. You must follow the passage away from the steps to find Angelus."

Then he took hold of Jax's arm and looked him in the eyes. "Don't judge your father too harshly. Ever since the death of your mother, he has been terrified that he might lose you too. Everything he has done since then has been to protect you."

Jax turned his head away angrily. "I don't believe that! He doesn't want to protect me that much if he's threatening to carry out the Spell of Removal on me!"

Valena waited until Jax turned his head back

again. Then he said gently, "Think of it this way. He would rather carry out the Spell of Removal than have you die and lose you forever." Jax opened his mouth to argue, then considered what Valena had said. "But without magic, I would only be half-alive," he whispered.

Valena shook his head. "I didn't say Revus was right. I just asked you not to judge him for the choices he has made."

He urged them onto the spellstation, and moved backwards to allow Jax to activate the symbols. As they prepared to step through the portal, Jax and Shannon held hands. Without warning, Shannon turned back to Valena. She could hardly see him through the shimmer created by the spellstation.

"Wait!" she said, raising her voice. "I have to ask you... can an underage magician carry out the Spell of Removal? Is it possible?"

Valena looked taken aback. "I don't know the answer to that. It has never been attempted of course. But the separation of underage magic is something that we created on Androva to exert control. It is likely that underage magicians could do any spell, if only we allowed it."

"Thank you," replied Shannon. "That's what I thought." Then, still holding hands, she and Jax walked through the portal to the other side.

It was very dark in the passageway. There was

only a faint light coming from the steps that Valena had described to them. It was also much colder. Shannon could feel the goose bumps on her arms as the damp air inside the mountain surrounded her. I miss my home, she thought desperately. I miss my old life. I don't want to do this. But she swallowed down her fear and held Jax's hand more tightly.

They stepped away from the light, deeper into the mountain. Jax kept one hand touching the wall to guide them along. All he could hear was the sound of their quick fearful breaths and the beating of his own heart, which was getting faster and faster. He wasn't sure if Shannon was the one who was trembling, or if it was him.

They inched further forward. Suddenly, out of the darkness, came a dreadful scream. Jax and Shannon both jumped, their anxiety turning to horror in an instant. Then came the sound of running footsteps, and a few seconds later someone collided with them, nearly knocking Shannon off her feet. The person made to run past them, but Jax managed to grab onto an arm to stop them.

"What is going on?" he whispered urgently. "Who are you and where did that noise come from?"

At first, there was only the sound of sobbing in response. Then the man spoke, though it came out more like a wail. "We have to go! We have to go now! He is escaping, Angelus is escaping!"

Jax and Shannon could feel the terror coming off the man in waves, and fought the temptation to start running away with him. "How is he escaping? What's happening?" Jax tried again.

"The harvested magic, it's disappearing, and it's all turning black! Paul and Celina, the other custodians, they tried to stop it, but as soon as their magic touched the blackness, they were dead! We have to go now, we have to get help!" And with that, he pushed Jax to one side and ran past them.

For a moment, Jax and Shannon didn't know what to do. It sounded pretty bad. Then Jax whispered, "OK, so now we know. The Council will be too late. We'll never find out if their plan would have worked. We're on our own."

Shannon found that her breath was coming in shallow, terrified gasps. This was it then. The two of them against Angelus.

22 Evil Awakes

Jax found his fear easier to control now that the moment of truth had arrived. He realised there was no turning back if Androva was to stand any chance of escaping the Evil that had threatened it for so long. "We can do this," he insisted to Shannon, still whispering. "If we don't try to defeat him now, he might just kill us all anyway when he escapes from the mountain."

Shannon nodded, then realising that Jax could not see her clearly in the dark, she managed to murmur yes. What Jax said was true. She just wished that her legs felt a bit less like jelly, and that her hands weren't shaking quite so much.

"I think the blackness must be coming from the Death Spell," continued Jax. "We know that Angelus's magic is black, and if it killed those two custodians, then he is projecting the Death Spell. He must be determined that anyone who gets near enough to capture him again won't survive."

Shannon croaked another yes in response.

"So we have to find the room that he is being held in, and wait until he is completely free. We can't touch him while he is projecting the Death Spell. We have to wait until he stops. If we stay well hidden, we might manage to take him by surprise. OK?"

Shannon's mouth was so dry that she had to swallow before whispering her reply. "Yes, but what if my Spell of Immobility isn't strong enough? What if I can't do it?"

"I believe in you," replied Jax, taking her hands. Leaning forward, he kissed her. His lips were warm. Shannon's heart jumped again, this time in surprise.

Not how I imagined my first kiss, she thought. But before another moment had gone by, she was smiling. The time and the place might be rubbish, but the boy doing the kissing was just about perfect, she thought.

Jax nervously waited for Shannon to say something. "I believe in you too," she whispered.

After a moment, Jax reached out to touch the wall again to guide them on their way. Shannon stopped him, having just remembered something. "What's the signal?" she asked. Jax realised immediately what she meant, and for a moment he was horrified. How could he have forgotten that?

They needed a signal so that Jax would know when Shannon dropped her Spell of Immobility. At that exact moment, he would project the Spell of Removal. It had to be something that wouldn't give the game away to Angelus. So they decided Shannon would cough twice. The first cough would act as a warning to Jax to get ready, and on the second cough, she would drop her spell.

It was time to move. They had no idea how long the passageway was, but judging from how close the scream had sounded, they did not have too far to go. Before long, it began to get a bit lighter, and they could see each other's faces again. The light was coming from a half-open doorway up ahead. As they got closer, they could see two bodies lying in the passageway. Shannon gulped, realising they had to be the two custodians, Paul and Celina.

Jax was grateful for the light coming from the doorway. Imagine how awful it would have been if we'd tripped over those poor custodians, he thought. When he decided that he and Shannon were close enough, he pulled her to a stop beside him. Holding his hand up to show that she should stay where she was, he crept forward.

He looked cautiously around the edge of the doorframe and saw that the room was larger than he had expected it to be. It had obviously been carved out of the rock of the mountain, and the floor was quite irregular in places.

There was a small black cloud, about the size of three people, in the centre of the room. The light spilling out into the passage was coming from two round Illumination Spells that were attached to opposite corners. The walls were still partly covered with the blue haze of a Protection Spell, though this was quite ragged in places.

Turning back to Shannon, he beckoned her forward, then darted across the doorway. He took up position on the far side, while Shannon took his place on the near side. The black cloud was already noticeably smaller than it had been a few seconds ago. Shannon and Jax took it in turns to quickly glance into the room. Soon the shape of a person was visible through the cloud.

When Shannon took her next glance, she recoiled in shock. The face she had seen was twisted with hatred, and the eyes were blazing with rage. It was a dreadful sight. Jax saw her appalled expression and faltered. A noise came from the room, starting low and growling, building up into a roar of anger.

Jax and Shannon stood frozen with fear as the roar went on and on. Then it died away, to be replaced by a silence that was even more terrifying. Their eyes met, wide with horror, and then Jax clenched his fists. "Now!" he mouthed to Shannon.

They stepped forward together, Shannon's hands already half-way to projecting the spell. As soon as she got her bearings, she threw her magic outwards at the figure standing in the centre of the room. This time there was no measuring out of the spell. She used everything she had. Jax waited, looking back and forth between Shannon and Angelus, trying to figure out if the Spell of Immobility was working. He noticed that Angelus was tall and thin, with white hair and extremely wrinkled skin.

Though his posture was slightly stooped, like that of an old man, he vibrated with power. Jax and Shannon could almost see his magical force field like a black glimmer surrounding him. At first he made no reaction to their arrival.

Then his eyes snapped wide open with outrage. "What is this?" he said, in a voice that was thin and menacing. Shannon and Jax had expected him to shout after the roar they had heard just before. But this low voice was somehow scarier. "Children?" he continued. "*Children?* Am I not deserving of a more worthy opponent than *this?*"

He laughed, and it was a sinister, confident sound, making their skin crawl. "Alright, *children,*" he said. "If you want to play with me, then you must accept the consequences of the game." He tried to raise his hands, then stopped as he realised Shannon's spell was holding his magic in place.

Jax wanted to shout with relief. This was the first sign he had seen that her Spell of Immobility was working. Shannon was thankful too, though she tried not to show it. It was not like it had been against Marcus and Revus. She could not feel the spell travelling into Angelus's body. His magic was like tar. It felt heavy and bitter, and she was struggling to push the spell further through it.

But it was becoming easier as she got her fear under control. Inch by inch, Angelus was held more firmly in place. However, he did not seem concerned. His lips curled back from his teeth in a gruesome smile.

"I hope you have a better plan than this," he hissed. "I just escaped from a Spell of Immobility much more powerful than yours. What happens when you get too tired to continue? What happens when your concentration wavers? For you cannot keep this up forever. But *I can!*" he finished triumphantly.

Shannon tried to stay calm. She had to push the spell right back into his head. She wanted to freeze as much of his magic as possible. She hoped that he couldn't immediately go on the attack when she finally dropped the spell.

She glanced at Jax, who gave her the most

encouraging look he could manage. Angelus, seeing this, laughed again. "How wonderful. You actually care about each other. This might be a better game than I expected. Which order shall I kill you in, I wonder? Which of you would suffer the most by seeing the other die first?"

Jax glared at him, and he sneered. "I think you would suffer the most," he said to Jax. "Knowing that you failed to protect your courageous little friend, watching the light leave her eyes as she realises you did not save her."

"Don't listen to him," said Shannon angrily. "He's a coward and a bully. Without his stolen powers, he is nothing. Even his own brother turned against him."

Angelus snarled at her. "Brave words, little girl. I might kill you second after all. I will enjoy watching you beg for your life after you see how painfully your friend has died."

"*Shut up!*" said Shannon. And with that she made a huge effort to force the spell into Angelus. Finally it was done. Angelus made a low growling noise, but could no longer speak.

Shannon coughed. For a second, Jax panicked. I'm not ready! he wanted to shout. But there was no time, so he drew his magic together, formulating the spell in his mind. His Sygnus started to spin. He held his breath, waiting for the second cough. And then it came.

Though it all happened in a few seconds, it seemed to Shannon as if everything slowed down. She saw Jax lift his hands, and the glow of his Spell of Removal projected outwards. It had very jagged edges and looked like no spell that she had ever seen before.

Angelus, realising immediately that he was free, crouched down as if to avoid the Spell of Removal. He lifted his own hands, and with terrifying speed, a glittering black shadow raced towards Jax.

Shannon heard herself screaming "No!" and she desperately projected another Spell of Immobility, this time in Jax's direction. She was hoping that if she froze his magic, the Death Spell would not be able to kill him. She had to do enough to protect him, without stopping the Spell of Removal that he had projected. He looked at her, shocked, as her spell hit him just before the black shadow did.

Angelus bellowed with frustration, and she could see that the Spell of Removal had reached him. Spinning in her direction, he used all his remaining magic to send a Death Spell straight at her.

She turned her head to look back at Jax. Seeing that the black shadow was still hanging in front of him, she concentrated on keeping the Spell of Immobility in place. She had no magic left to protect herself. "I'm sorry," she whispered to Jax, smiling through her tears. And then she fell.

For a little while, there was silence in the room. The black clouds from the Death Spells gradually dissolved, followed by the silver glow of Shannon's Spell of Immobility. As soon as he could move again, Jax leapt to his feet.

He rushed to Shannon, who was lying back on the stone floor as if she were asleep. Frantically Jax lifted her head onto his lap and tried to wake her up. "Shannon, please!" he begged. "Please open your eyes. Please!"

Shannon remained motionless. "Help!" Jax shouted. "Somebody help me!"

There was no answer. "Somebody help me," he repeated more quietly, and a single tear fell down his face and landed on Shannon's cheek.

Eventually Jax remembered Angelus. A trembling figure was hunched over in the far corner. Without his magic to sustain him, Angelus was nothing but a frail old man, and he was absolutely terrified.

Jax gathered himself together long enough to project a basic Protection Spell around Angelus, just to make sure he didn't wander off before the Council decided what to do with him. Then he turned back to Shannon, smoothing her hair back off her forehead.

"I won't leave you," he promised, but

Shannon did not answer.

23 Afterwards

The minutes gradually passed, and Jax began to hear voices approaching along the passageway. Stupid, he thought. If Angelus still had his magic, they would all be dead as soon as he heard them. As the voices got closer, Jax could hear that they were raised in disagreement. Then the first two people appeared at the doorway.

They were both members of the Council. Seeing Jax and Shannon, and Angelus in the corner whimpering to himself, their voices trailed off, and their mouths fell open in shock. More people appeared behind them, until eventually there were seven magicians in total, each falling silent when they understood what they were seeing. Jax didn't have the energy to speak, so he decided to keep his eyes on Shannon and just ignore them.

The last to arrive was Valena, the young magician who had helped Jax and Shannon earlier. He seemed less shell-shocked than the others. Within a few seconds he had recovered himself enough to walk across the room to confirm that Angelus was no longer a threat. Then he went to Jax, and crouching down alongside him and Shannon, he gently asked Jax to tell him what had happened.

In a weary voice, Jax explained. Every so often, his voice would fade away as he looked back down at Shannon. When he got to the part where Shannon had sacrificed herself to keep him safe, he struggled to complete the story. After he finally got to the end, Valena rested his hand on Jax's shoulder for a moment in silent sympathy.

Then Valena raised his head and addressed the other magicians. "You all heard what happened here. Our world is now free of the Evil that terrorised it for so long. And it is thanks to this boy and this girl that we are now safe. We are in their debt. From this moment, their bravery will echo down the years of Androva's history."

Getting to his feet, he continued. "Go back to Landor and tell the others. Our world will rejoice at this new freedom."

At first Jax thought he had misheard Valena. His expression was incredulous. "Rejoice? We can't rejoice when Shannon is *dead*!"

Valena turned back to Jax in surprise. "No, she

is not," he contradicted. Valena and Jax stared at each other for a moment, then Jax's expression wavered. He hardly dared to hope.

"What do you mean, she is not?" he asked. "She took a direct hit from the Death Spell!"

"Yes, she did. But you told me that your Spell of Removal had already reached Angelus. Therefore gaps would have started to appear in his magic. Even if his spark was still in place, once the Spell of Removal has been started, there is no going back. The internal connections begin to fail immediately. You cannot project a complete spell."

Jax sat still, absorbing this information. "Then why won't she wake up?" he challenged.

"An incomplete spell can still do some damage," replied Valena. "She will wake up soon, I'm sure. Look," he added, pointing to Shannon. "I can already see that her face is less pale."

Jax looked down at Shannon, and saw that Valena was right. Even as he watched, her eyelids fluttered, not quite opening, but definitely moving. He closed his own eyes to get his feelings under control, not wanting to cry in front of everyone.

"I don't believe it," he whispered to himself. He had experienced such grief when he thought that Shannon had been killed by Angelus, that it was taking him a moment to accept that everything was OK.

Suddenly, running footsteps could be heard coming down the passage. Revus appeared in the doorway, wild-eyed with panic. He came to a halt at the sight of Jax and Shannon. It seemed to take him several moments to absorb the fact that Jax was unharmed. He sagged against the door frame, and his face showed that he was struggling to hold back his emotions.

At first Jax watched Revus coldly, unimpressed by the sight of his father after what had happened in the Assembly. Then, as he saw that Revus was genuinely beside himself with relief, Jax softened. "All is well, Father," he said kindly.

"What happened here?" Revus stammered, finally able to speak.

Valena smiled. "I think Jax should tell you. Your son and the girl are heroes," he confirmed. "In the meantime, ladies and gentlemen, I think we should deal with this pathetic creature in the corner, don't you?"

Excited murmuring had broken out amongst the other magicians. Angelus was led away, still whimpering. Gradually the atmosphere lightened as the years of accumulated fear fell away. Faces that had been tense with dread started to relax. Several magicians approached Jax to congratulate him.

More and more Androvans arrived in the

passageway as the news spread, wanting to see for themselves that the room where Angelus had been held all these years was definitely harmless again. Jax tried to tell his father exactly what had happened to them. And then, finally, Shannon woke up.

She had been listening to the voices for a little while, feeling as if she were in a dream, knowing that she wanted to open her eyes, but not quite able to manage it. Where am I? she thought, unable to remember exactly what had taken place. Then it all came back to her in a big rush, and she gasped, sitting bolt upright with shock.

"Ow!" yelled Jax, clutching his face. Shannon had sat up so unexpectedly that she had smacked his cheekbone with her forehead, and rather hard too. She looked at him in surprise, still getting her bearings, and he started to laugh. "You're awake then?" he joked. Shannon frowned and looked round the room, confused at seeing all the people.

Most were looking at her with happy faces, and a few even clapped. "Angelus?" she asked tentatively.

"Finished," said Jax, with a broad smile. "His magic is completely gone. He's just a feeble old man. The Council will handle him now."

"I thought…" began Shannon shakily. "I thought he was going to kill me."

A shadow passed over Jax's face. "For a while, it looked as if he had," he replied.

They stared into each other's eyes for a moment, and then Shannon smiled and flung her arms around him. "So we did it then? We actually did it? I can't believe it, I can't believe it! That's totally amazing!"

Jax laughed again as he hugged her back. Revus watched them, smiling faintly. Now that the drama was over, he was already thinking ahead about how to manage the repercussions. Angelus was defeated, but the problem of Shannon's magical ability still remained. Should the Code be rewritten? They needed to protect themselves against the risk that another Angelus could be created in the future.

And how to deal with Shannon's return to Terra? She could not be allowed to tell anyone about her experiences on Androva. Revus was far from happy.

When they returned to Landor, the streets were full of delighted Androvans. Despite the lateness of the hour, everyone was determined to celebrate their freedom, and excited chattering could be heard from one end of the capital to the other. Lights were shining in every house, food and drink were being shared generously with passers-by, and Firework Spells were illuminating the sky.

Shannon found it incredible. Androva seemed like a different world to the one she had seen previously. Their progress through Landor was slow, as everyone wanted to thank them. The story of how Angelus had been overpowered was getting more exaggerated each time it was told.

Shannon noticed that the travel through the portal back to Landor had not made her tired this time. She had also been fine on the way to the mountain, though obviously she had not paid attention at the time. She was just wondering if she recognised the street that Darius's house was on, when someone ran into her and Jax and hugged them both.

It was Darius, so delighted to see them that he could hardly speak at first. But once the three friends started talking, there was no stopping them.

Iona and Marek were waiting at their door, their faces soft and happy. It was agreed that Jax and Shannon would spend the rest of the night with them. They had no desire to go back to Mabre House and its dark, gloomy rooms. The celebration continued into the early hours. When Iona eventually insisted that they all go to bed, no one protested. The lack of sleep was catching up with everyone, and it would be their first decent rest for several days and nights.

Revus was up early, as he intended to call

another Council Assembly. He wished to regain control of the situation as quickly as possible. Fortunately for Jax and Shannon, and in fact everyone on Androva, the Council's collective opinion had changed. Most were now convinced that Androva did not need as many rules and regulations as before. Indeed, argued some, it could be said that the recent epidemic of rule breaking was the reason that Androva was now free from the Evil.

No one was suggesting that there should be no rules at all. Only that life on Androva should be less restricted. "Just imagine," said Valena, "if the Foundation for Research had been rebuilt after the Evil was first contained. Perhaps we could have found a way to defeat Angelus hundreds of years ago!"

It was decided that the Council would meet in one week to propose a new Code. The objective would be to protect its magicians and the world they lived in, but at the same time to inspire them. Shannon would be allowed to return home with her magic ability intact. Androva would not try to control what happened next.

Revus accepted that he was beaten. Valena took him to one side after the Assembly finished. "Open your heart, my friend," said Valena gently. "Let go of your fear, and you might find that you win back your son."

When Jax and Shannon heard what had happened at the Assembly, they could hardly believe it. They had been waiting anxiously with Darius, and were sitting having a very late breakfast when Revus returned.

"You mean I can still be a magician?" asked Shannon, a smile spreading across her face. "We can be friends?" she said to Jax and Darius. "You can travel to my world, and I can travel to yours?" She was hardly able to sit still in her excitement. "This is going to be awesome!" Jax and Darius smiled back at her, enjoying her enthusiasm.

Then Jax glanced at his father, who had delivered the news in a rather subdued tone. Revus looked back at him uncertainly. He was not sure how to treat Jax now. Jax gave his father a nod, his eyes warm, and Revus smiled in relief. He hoped that this would be a new beginning for both of them.

Jax turned back to Shannon and Darius, who were making lots of plans for the future. Shannon said she really wanted to learn how to control her ability. She asked what school was like on Androva. Darius wanted to find out more about Terra and what life was like if you weren't a magician.

"I can't wait to show you!" answered Shannon. "We might not have magic, but we have some pretty cool stuff even so. Mobile phones, aeroplanes, chocolate! I don't even know where to start!"

Jax listened to Shannon and Darius for a few minutes, until Shannon noticed that he was staying quiet.

"What do you want to do?" she asked him.

"Oh, I just want to hang out with you for a while. Maybe finish reading that book you lent me. Everything else is a bonus." There was a smile in his green eyes that made her heart jump again, and she grinned back at him. I might have a boyfriend, she thought. Penny will never believe it. I'm not sure I believe it myself.

A short time later, having said goodbye to Darius, Shannon and Jax returned to the portal room in Mabre House. Before they stepped onto the spellstation, Revus awkwardly patted Shannon on the arm and cleared his throat.

"I never thanked you for what you did," he said, embarrassed. "You saved my son's life, and I will be forever grateful to you." Shannon put her hand over his for a moment, to show him that she appreciated his words. Then she and Jax turned around, and Jax activated the symbols. Once the shimmer had risen high enough to cover them both, they stepped forward.

It was another sunny afternoon in Shannon's garden, and she blinked at the brightness. She realised that it had to be Wednesday already. Two nights had passed since the Monday afternoon when Marcus had collected her. She looked at Jax questioningly, wondering if he was going to stay or return to Androva straight away. He shook his head.

"I think I'll save the big introductions for another time," he said. "You should probably find out if Aaron's Distraction Spell is still working OK before you show up with a complete stranger."

Shannon agreed. Now that she knew she would definitely see Jax again, she didn't mind him going back. "See you soon, Shannon," he promised. Pulling her towards him, he closed his eyes and kissed her, and this time Shannon kissed him back. Then Jax walked through the portal. Smiling, her cheeks pink, Shannon watched him disappear. She reluctantly made her way into the house, a bit nervous about what she might find.

"Oh, there you are Shannon," said her mother in a matter-of-fact voice as she stepped into the hallway. "I wondered where you'd got to. Are you going to finish your homework or not? You'll have to go back to school tomorrow—you've already missed too many days."

Shannon hesitated for a moment, astonished. Her mother was behaving as if she had just been in the next room all this time! *I guess the*

Distraction Spell worked pretty well, she thought.

"Well, don't just stand there," said her mother, slightly cross. "Homework, remember! It's not going to get done by magic."

Shannon laughed. Under her breath, she said, "You might be in for a surprise there…"

The Legacy of Androva Series
Continues...

It's your average new school nightmare. Classes you've never taken, teachers you've never met before. Having to pass a really difficult entrance exam. Oh, and upsetting the most popular girl in the school before you've even arrived.

Except this school is the Seminary of Magic on Androva. A world you only discovered a few weeks ago. You're a brand-new magician, with a brand-new boyfriend, and unfortunately you're about to discover a brand new enemy, who will stop at nothing to get their hands on some magic.

But how do you know whom you can trust? If you get it wrong, you might end up paying with your life...

Jax and Shannon are back in *Capturing Magic*, and things are getting complicated!

You can find out more about the author, and the rest of the books in the Legacy of Androva series, at
www.alexcvick.com

Made in the USA
San Bernardino, CA
01 March 2020